The Three Mrs. Monroes Trilogy

Vivian

book three

by
Bernadette Marie

This is a fictional work. The names, characters, incidents, places, and locations are solely the concepts and products of the author's imagination or are used to create a fictitious story and should not be construed as real.

5 PRINCE PUBLISHING AND BOOKS, LLC

PO Box 16507
Denver, CO 80216
www.5PrinceBooks.com

ISBN 13: 978-1-63112-043-5 ISBN 10:1631120433
VIVIAN
Bernadette Marie
Copyright Bernadette Marie 2014
Published by 5 Prince Publishing

Front Cover Viola Estrella

First Edition/First Printing September 2014 Printed U.S.A.

5 PRINCE PUBLISHING AND BOOKS, LLC.

BERNADETTE MARIE

Coming 2015
The Walkers

To Stan,
The one who leads me to all healing by being by my side.

Acknowledgements

To Stan and our boys who make every pain I ever have (physical or emotional) go away because of your love.

To Mom, Dad, and Sissy, your love and support is immeasurable! Thank you for it!

To Connie, Clare, Marie, and Grace, you literally keep track of all my pieces and make sure they fall back into place. You are glorious women!

To June thank you for being you. Thank goodness this isn't our last year together!

To my Street Team and Beta Readers, you continue to inspire me with your love and support!

Dear Reader,

Here we are at the conclusion of the Monroes.

What a wonderful journey I have had with these three women. I hope you have enjoyed them as much as I have.

In the final installment, we see the rise of Vivian. For so long, she's been the angry, bitter, moody side of the Monroes. Now we begin to see her soften with the love of a good man who sees a silver lining in everything.

I hope you enjoy Vivian. I fell in love with her writing this.

What's next for me? Follow me on Facebook and Twitter and you'll be the first in line to see the progress of my new family series coming 2015.

Happy Reading,
Bernadette Marie

Vivian

Chapter One

God she was miserable. Vivian Monroe sat in her car just on the outskirts of town. The late November wind was kicking up. It was cold and her damn car had stalled—just like everything had for her for years.

It had been less than six months ago that she found out her husband of ten years had married two other women before his death.

Never in a million years, though, did she think she'd make a new life with those other two Mrs. Monroes. Adam, her late husband, had left her with nothing. His second wife, whom he'd left everything to, had stepped up to make sure that Vivian and her daughters were always taken care of. She may never admit it aloud, but she'd learned a lot from Amelia.

It had been Amelia who had come up with the plan for Adam's widows to take what he'd left and start a business. It would help to take care of Adam's children and then no one walked away with everything. They were building a daycare center of all things. It would open next week if everything went according to plan.

Her mind shifted to Penelope, Adam's newest wife. Though Penelope was only ten years, or so, younger than her, she felt as if she were a mother to the girl. Penelope was eight months pregnant with Adam's baby. She needed compassion—especially from Vivian, who'd been through the process.

Vivian gritted her teeth and tried to start the engine again. Nothing.

She'd called for help, but it was going to be awhile. Sam, her late husband's lawyer and Amelia's new fiancé, was in court. Amelia had an inspector at the old house they were

VIVIAN

converting into the daycare center. And Penelope and Brock, the man who had been by Adam's side when he died in combat and now was Penelope's fiancé, were in a doctor's appointment.

She was totally alone. Even her own girls were at the rec center daycare for the day. That, she thought, was the only plus to the day.

The day trip to Oklahoma City to find out anything she could on Adam's mother hadn't turned up much. Stella Monroe, by all accounts, seemed to be missing.

Vivian hated that she thought it wasn't really a bad thing to have the woman MIA. But, it did mean they didn't know where she was and there was a great chance she'd be coming after her.

After Adam had died, her mother-in-law had, well, gone off the deep end. Her husband had even found it beneficial to move her to Florida and away from Parson's Gulch, Oklahoma where she'd made her home for most of her life.

Still, she'd texted Vivian three weeks ago saying she was coming after her and then the house where they were building the daycare had been broken into. Things just weren't adding up.

Vivian smiled when she thought about the books that had been thrown around in the attic the night of the break in. They'd all been full of money. Six thousand dollars had been found in between the pages and in the cutouts of the vintage books. Adam's grandmother had stashed it all there. As far as she was concerned, when they were given the house and all of its contents that included the money too. Of course, now sitting in her broken down car meant it might have to be used for costly repairs.

Another car pulled up behind hers, but it wasn't one of the four people she'd called. She looked into the review mirror and saw Clayton North stepping out of his car.

Great. The one man who had turned her head in all these years had come to rescue her. He and that shiny gold band on his hand that she'd neglected to see the first day she'd met him.

Oh, she had to have looked stupid flirting with him like she was. What made her think he was available? And why did she care, except she'd gotten caught up in all this falling in love that had been going on. First Amelia and Sam and then Penelope and Brock. She was a woman after all. She could certainly blame it on hormones.

She let out a long breath and waited for him to come to her door. When he tapped on the window, she opened the door.

"It's so dead I can't roll down the window," she said, forcing a smile on her face.

"I brought cables. I'll give you a jump."

"Thanks." She popped the hood of her car, climbed out, and watched as Clayton walked back and climbed into his car. He drove it around the quiet road so that he was parked right next to her.

He popped the hood of his car as he climbed out. "It'll just take a moment."

He pulled the cables out of his car and walked around to the front of the cars.

Clayton chuckled to himself. "I always forget which way these go."

"Red ones are positive. Black are negative."

He nodded. "Right. You'd think that would be easy enough to remember."

VIVIAN

Clayton went about connecting the cables and Vivian watched, then what he said hit her.

"You said you brought cables. You didn't just have them and saw me stranded?"

Clayton shook his head. "The gal at the front desk of the rec center lent them to me. I'd gone to get my girls and they said you'd called because you were going to be late. I told them I'd come get you."

Vivian nodded slowly, her stare fixed on this man she'd flirted with and even had invited to a private bar-b-cue. She sickened herself. Though he did come without his wife. That didn't uphold his character very well, she decided.

"You drove all the way out here to get me?"

"Yes."

"Why?"

Clayton looked around and then back at her. "Because you're stranded."

She crossed her arms over her chest as much out of irritation as to shield her from the cold. "Just a nice guy routine?"

Clayton's sandy hair was blowing in the opposite direction in which he'd combed it, giving it a ledge. His brown eyes were narrowed on her as he held the last cord in his hand.

"No routine going on. I thought we were friends and you needed some help."

"Friends? I just met you a few weeks ago."

"Right." He winced. "You invited me to a party too. Friends do that. Even if they just met. Remember I'm new in town. I don't know too many people."

"Whatever. Thanks for coming out. Very strange, but thank you." She couldn't even stand the sound of her own voice as she talked to him. The first time they'd met she was giddy and gushy—not like her either. But now she was being crude and snide. More like her, she thought, but not nice.

He clamped the last cable to the side of the engine compartment. "Okay, go start your car."

Vivian walked back to her car and turned the key. The car sputtered and finally came to life. When she looked up Clayton stood there with an enormous grin looking down at two running engines.

That nerdy grin was making her insides gooey again, just as it had when he'd arrived at the old house looking for a daycare for his girls. Two of the cutest girls she'd ever seen.

It was stupid to be mad at herself just because an attractive, smart guy considered her a friend. And then there was the matter of fact that he was going to be paying some of her bills when his daughters attended their daycare.

She let her mouth slide into an easy smile as she climbed out of the car.

"I really appreciate you coming to help me out. That was above and beyond."

"I'd like to think that someone would help me someday too."

Cute and genuinely nice. His wife was a lucky lady— whoever she was.

Clayton took the cables off of the batteries and rolled them around his arm. Vivian slammed down her hood and he did the same.

"Amelia is with the inspector now getting everything signed off on the daycare. If everything goes well, we should be open next week."

His eyes grew wide. "Oh, that'll be great. My girls talk about your girls non-stop. They'll be glad to be around them all the time."

VIVIAN

He was easy to look at and easy to talk to. She found herself wanting to do just that—stare and talk.

"How is school going?" she asked, remembering that he was a new school teacher in town.

"So far, not bad. I've been called Mr. South, Mr. West, Mr. East, and Mr. Northbound."

She chuckled and he eased his hip against his car, which only made him cuter.

"Third graders are funny like that."

"Sometimes sassier than high schoolers."

When he crossed his arms over his chest, she was reminded of that wedding ring on his finger. She didn't want to be that other woman to worry about.

Vivian pushed back her shoulders and held out her hand. "Thank you, Mr. Northwest, for helping me out today."

He grinned as he shook her hand. "My pleasure."

"I look forward to seeing the girls next week."

She turned back to her car and began to climb inside.

"Hey," he called. "I'm taking the fam out for pizza on Saturday night. That place on the edge of town with the video games."

She nodded. She knew the place too well. That was where she and Adam had spent many of their teenage lustful nights.

"Anyway," he continued. "Why don't you and the girls meet us there? We can have family pizza night for everyone."

Vivian swallowed hard. "They'd like that."

He gave her a wave as he climbed into his car and motioned for her to drive ahead of him.

She put the car in gear and started back down the road.

Looking back in her rearview mirror, she saw him on his cell phone. No doubt talking to his wife.

She was a big enough woman to be friends with him—and the wife. She'd been lied to and she didn't trust anyone, so this would be a good step for her. Trust a man she just met that makes her insides gooey—and spend time with his kids and wife.

Nothing seemed off about that at all, she tried to convince herself. He was just a good, decent man. He'd come to her rescue and his daughters would be in her care next week when her business opened.

But it didn't stop the fact that he was so handsome and she wished he was single.

Chapter Two

Vivian had stopped for a few groceries before picking up her girls from the rec center daycare. There was undoubtedly some thrill in knowing that they wouldn't have to go there next week, for her anyway.

The entire reason they'd decided to open a daycare center was so Vivian and Penelope could have their children with them at all times.

As she and the girls walked through the lobby, Amelia peeked her head out of the gymnasium doors. She'd been teaching self-defense and kickboxing there since July. And even though there was work for her at the daycare, Vivian was sure she'd never give up her teaching. It was part of who Amelia was—one bad ass girl.

"Hey, I wanted to tell you that we passed all our inspections!"

Vivian let out a deep breath. "I didn't doubt it but I sure feel better knowing it."

Amelia smiled. "Sam picked up a bottle of champagne and some sparkling cider for Penelope and the girls. We thought we'd celebrate tonight over at the house."

Vivian nodded as Amelia ducked back into the gym. She'd really wanted to just go home and soak in her tub, but it looked like she'd be heading over to the old house they'd remodeled to celebrate the opening of the daycare.

After a glass of champagne, she'd head home to soak in a tub full of bubbles that went up to her eyebrows. The thought made her smile. She'd have to make sure the girls were asleep first, or she'd have company.

VIVIAN

When she pulled up in front of the old house, she was more than surprised to see Clayton carrying things out of it.

"Mommy, they're here!" Emma screamed from the back seat, loud enough it made Vivian wince.

"Yes, honey, they are." But why were they there?

Vivian stepped out of the car and opened the back doors to unbuckle her girls. They wiggled free, jumped from the car, and she watched them run off and into the house.

Clayton gave her a wave. "Your girls couldn't get here fast enough. Stephanie has been asking about them for a half hour—nonstop."

"Why are you here?"

Again her words sounded curt and nasty. What was it about this man? To look at him set her insides to goo and then she'd talk and nothing but ugly came out.

"I ran into Sam at the rec center. He takes yoga," he said quietly as if maybe no one was supposed to know.

"He's really good at it. It keeps him calm."

Clayton considered it. "Maybe I'll be wanting to look into that before the end of the school year." He laughed and wouldn't you know it—that was sexy too. "He said he and Brock could use a hand moving some things out of here."

Brock walked out of the door with a suitcase and hoisted it into the back of his truck.

"What is all that?" Vivian asked.

"Penelope's stuff. I think it's time she moved in with me. The baby looks to only be a few weeks away." He was grinning and beaming, she noted. The man was as giddy for this baby to arrive as he was to marry a woman that Vivian should absolutely despise—but she loved her instead.

"I just thought we were going to wait a bit."

Brock shrugged. "Sam hired a guy to start on that other bedroom next week." Brock held up a hand as she took a breath to protest. "He'll be working after business hours. Sam knows the responsibility for those who will come in and out of the house. It'll take a few weeks longer, but then you and the girls can move in there."

They'd discussed Vivian moving into the old house for convenience. After all, she'd been living in a borrowed townhouse for months since her house had been lost in a late summer tornado. She hadn't really talked to Sam about it, but she figured the man who had let him use it for her and the girls was probably wanting to rent it out.

"I suppose I should prepare them for another move," she looked toward the house where she could see little girls running back and forth from room to room.

"I could help you move too if you need it," Clayton offered. "I don't think you can ever have too many hands when moving." He smiled again.

"You're very generous with your time."

"It's something I can give freely." He wiped his hands on his pant legs. "I'm off for another box."

She watched him walk away—perhaps too intently. When he'd disappeared through the door, she turned toward Brock.

"Why did Sam ask him to help?"

"They talked a lot at the barbeque a few weeks ago. When he saw him today, he invited him over. He is, after all, your first paying customer—for lack of a better word."

"Don't you think it's funny how he just shows up everywhere, but his wife doesn't?"

Brock shrugged his shoulders. "Maybe he got the job here and she hasn't come along yet. I've never seen a woman with him."

"Neither have I, but he wears a ring. I just think it's odd."

"Have you asked him?"

VIVIAN

Vivian gasped as if she were shocked by his question. "No. It's none of my business."

"Then don't worry about it. He's a great guy and the girls love his girls. We can all use a new friend."

She had somehow surrounded herself with people who were too damn optimistic.

Most of Penelope's things were packed into Brock's truck before Amelia had arrived. With the laughter of little girls running through Penelope's now empty bedroom, the six adults stood in the old 70's décor kitchen and popped the top to the champagne. Sam filled five plastic champagne glasses with champagne and one with sparkling cider for Penelope. They all raised them in a toast.

No one spoke for a beat and then Amelia chuckled to herself.

"It might seem like the worst time for this, but a toast to Adam Monroe. Had his mama not screwed him up, we wouldn't all be here today."

Each of them laughed, except for Clayton, who was respectfully quiet. He probably had no idea who Adam Monroe was.

The bubbles went straight to Vivian's head and she winced from the bite that champagne always gave her. It was then she'd remembered she hadn't eaten lunch. She had groceries wasting away in the car. And if she had one more sip from that glass she might have to crash on a nap mat in the toddler room.

She set the glass down on the counter. "I should get home. I haven't eaten all day. I can't have any more of this."

Penelope dropped her shoulders and a pout formed on her bottom lip. "Don't go yet. I made dinner."

"You did?" Vivian looked around the kitchen. She didn't see anything or smell it.

"It's at Brock's in the slow cooker." She turned her pout toward him, only now she batted her lashes. "Will you go get it? There is wrapped corn bread on the counter too."

"Did you plan to feed this many people?" he asked with an adoring grin on his face.

"I made way too much. Please go get it."

Brock caressed her cheek and nodded. "I'll be back in twenty minutes."

Vivian felt like a kid who had been drug to an adult function. The adults wouldn't quit talking and all she wanted to do was go home and soak in that tub.

Penelope sat down at the table and picked up her cell phone. She'd been wedding planning for three weeks and at every free moment she was looking on Pinterest for the perfect post-baby dress.

Sam and Amelia were in mid banter about their own wedding as they moved about the kitchen.

That left her standing awkwardly silent with Clayton. Vivian picked up her glass. "I think I'll drink this on the front porch."

The girls were all still giggling as she walked down the hall and out the door. She sat in one of the two rocking chairs on the front porch and turned when she heard the screen door open. She hadn't invited Clayton to join her, but she wasn't surprised to find him walking toward the empty seat next to her either.

The night was dark and chilly. She'd need to remember to start keeping heavier coats in the car.

"It's a clear night," Clayton said as he looked out to the sky rocking his chair with one foot. "You didn't get stars like this in the city."

Ah, he was opening up. Vivian took a sip from her glass and thought she'd see what she could pull out of him.

VIVIAN

"What city?"

"Seattle."

He'd come further than she'd thought. "I've never been there."

"You should go. It's a nice place. But not enough jobs for teachers in the area I was looking. Besides, this is better for the girls right now."

"You're licensed in both states?"

He nodded as he looked down into his glass. "When Linda and I were first married we moved around a lot. One of those places happened to be outside of Tulsa." He smiled in the dim light. "I could teach in Kansas too if I wanted to."

She had a name. Linda was his wife and they'd moved around a lot. She had a sense of loss. She'd moved away with Adam once and she was miserable. Who knew that would always have been the norm.

"My degree is in early childhood development," she said. "I never really got to use it—until now."

Clayton took a sip of his drink. "Do you mind if I ask, about Adam Monroe...someone's husband? Relative?"

Vivian winced.

"The toast in there?"

He shrugged. "I've heard the name a few times. And I've seen the list at the rec center. You and Amelia have the same last name. I just figured you must all be related somehow."

Related wasn't really the word for it.

She let out a breath as she contemplated isolating herself from this man—Linda's husband. Or would he pull the enrollment of his daughters? She was going to walk a slippery slope no matter what she told him.

"Let's establish a few things before I tell you about Adam Monroe."

"O-kay," he drew out the word slowly.

"I would assume you came to Brock's barbeque, you saved my ass on the side of the road today, and you're here moving boxes because you consider all of us friends."

"I'm pretty sure I made that clear today on the side of the road."

"Well, let's establish some business items. You're leaving your girls in my care. You'll be paying me to do so, therefore, my livelihood will depend on you keeping your girls here."

"Right," again he drew out the word. "I'm worried now, I hope you understand that."

"I'm worried too." But she decided to dive in and tell him about the man he'd asked about. "Adam Monroe was my husband."

"Was."

"He died in combat in July."

Clayton's eyes opened wide and he reached a hand to her and rested it on her arm. "I'm so sorry. I had no idea."

"High school sweethearts. You know, the whole thing. Ten years of marriage and two girls."

"It's devastating."

"It was. We'd grown apart. In the past two years, I hadn't seen him but maybe once." She sipped from her glass. She needed the liquid courage to continue. "Come to find out the reason I hadn't had any contact with my husband in years was because of his mother. She'd stolen all of the letters that came from him."

"Why would she...sorry. That's none of my business."

"It's okay. I want to ask her the same thing."

"You haven't spoken to her?"

"Not in awhile. But I will." She bit down on the inside of her cheek to remind herself to not make her night about Stella Monroe. She was going to find out about Linda and Clayton. But to get to that point she had to keep talking.

VIVIAN

"Anyway, in one of those letters he asked me for a divorce—since I obviously was blowing him off."

"He seriously thought you had done that?"

"Yep. And he married Amelia."

That had taken the wind out of the man. He sat there silently obviously taking in what she'd said.

"So he had two wives."

"He did until Amelia found out about me, asked for a divorce and before it was final he'd married Penelope."

There. It was out. Now he knew their dirty little secret and he was silent.

Vivian was prepared for the words *I'd better be going* or *I think I'm going to keep the girls at the rec center*. But he said nothing. Instead, he kept his hand on her arm.

"You must have been shocked." His voice was calm and cool and his hand hadn't left her arm.

"I suppose you could say that."

"So the three of you," he thought for a moment, "are all friends?"

"We've become friends."

"You didn't know them before?"

She shook her head. "No. We met after his funeral in Sam's office. They were both at the funeral, though I didn't know about Penelope yet."

Now the hand that still rested on her arm moved across her skin in a soothing rub. "Sam. Where does he fit in? He's engaged to Amelia, right?"

She nodded slowly, soaking in the feeling of his touch and trying hard to accept it as a friendly gesture and nothing more. "He was Adam's lawyer."

Another slow nod, but judgment didn't cloud his eyes— only concentration.

"They fell in love then?"

"Yes. Very lucky couple."

"Penelope? I assume the baby is Adam's?"

Vivian bit down on her bottom lip and nodded. "Adam met her and married her two weeks later. She got pregnant and he got deployed and died."

Now his fingers stopped their stroking and he gave her a gentle squeeze. "How are you dealing with that?"

She wanted to be honest with him. Something inside of her said she should. After all, since that day they told her Adam died and the next day when she'd found out about Amelia she'd never had anyone to talk to.

Her entire body tensed and her breath stuck in her chest. Tears would come next, she knew that, and they did.

"No one's really asked me that before." She put her hand on her chest to calm her heartbeat, which had started to race when she thought about how she felt. "It's just something I deal with. Please don't get me wrong. Since we've all become more like sisters, I'm very excited for her. The girls are happy to have a sister or brother, but…" The sobbing started. "But my husband made that baby while he lied to me. He was my husband first. The father of my children first. I was to accept he died and left three wives?"

Her heart hurt. Her body ached. Clayton's hand held her arm tighter. "Let it out. It's okay."

"It's not okay. It's not okay to be mad anymore." She pulled her arm from his touch and wiped her eyes with both hands. "I love them. They are my sisters now. My family. I can't be mad. I can't." She stood from her chair and he from his.

"You can be. Inside you are. It doesn't mean you hate or you have bad feelings toward them, but it's okay for you to let it go like this."

VIVIAN

She shook her head. "No. No. It's not okay." She wiped her hands on her thighs. "Thank you for the talk. I need to get home."

And with that, she turned and walked back into the house to gather her girl and go home. Penelope's dinner would have to be missed. Vivian needed to escape to that bubble bath right now.

Chapter Three

When the house was quiet and he'd gotten two restless and tired girls bathed and to sleep, Clayton sat down at his desk and buried his face in his hands.

It was ten o'clock and he had papers to look over and planning to do. Not to mention he had a load of laundry molding in the washer he'd forgotten to dry. A sink full of dishes were calling for him to attend to. The bathtub needed to be washed out from all the soap the girls used during bath time. But he couldn't focus on that right now. He was too focused on Vivian.

Burned in his mind were those dark, sad eyes and that velvet skin under his fingertips. When she'd started to cry her lips had swollen into a pink pout and he'd fought off every urge to kiss them.

It wasn't his place to move into territory he didn't understand. He wouldn't have wanted that either. But Vivian Monroe needed some help. She needed someone to talk to. It had helped him when he'd needed it. In hindsight, he realized he hadn't been too open to the concept either. He just had to find a way to convince her to take the help.

She didn't have to accept what her late husband did. She didn't have to pretend to not be angry either.

It was completely obvious that Vivian loved Amelia and Penelope like sisters. They'd all take care of each other and stand up for each other. But he wondered, after her breakdown tonight, had she ever let it out?

But then when would there have been time, he wondered. If her husband died in July and it was easing out of November, when had she had time to mourn or get angry?

Perhaps she thought she'd done that all those years he wasn't around—all that time when he was marrying other people.

What kind of man did that?

His head throbbed thinking about it. A man who didn't know his place in the world—that's who.

Vivian hadn't gone into it much, but if it were his mother that truly caused this mess, then what kind of mess was her late husband? Certainly a mother like that wouldn't have raised a child full of good consciousness.

His heart ached for Adam Monroe. He'd given his life for his country and he'd left three angry, heartbroken women behind—and their children.

Amelia seemed to have coped and moved on. If he didn't know about Adam Monroe, he'd never have known that she'd been hurt. And Brock coddled Penelope in such a way that no one would ever assume that they'd not been a couple for a very long time.

Vivian should be as lucky to move on, he thought. But she'd need to find peace and when she broke down at his questions, he knew she wasn't at peace yet.

Was he?

Clayton leaned back in his chair and laced his fingers behind his head. Living in some small town with his little girls wasn't what he thought he'd be doing ten years ago. He and Linda had plans.

Travel the world. Teach the world. But things didn't always work out the way people planned them.

He rubbed his eyes and looked at the time. Somehow it was now nearly midnight and none of the things he needed to do had been done.

Clayton shut off the lamp on his desk. He'd get it done tomorrow. Now he was going to fall into bed and see if sleep would come at all. If he was lucky, he might get an hour before Stephanie was in his bed too. But he didn't blame her. He didn't like to be alone in his bed either.

~*~

The sun was too bright, Vivian thought as she drove from the townhouse she'd been staying in, to the old house on Main and Pine. The back of her car had suitcases piled in it. Suitcases of nonessential things that had been salvaged from the house after the tornado.

When she'd mentioned to the girls that Penelope was moving in with Brock and they'd move to the old house, the girls had been giddy. They couldn't wait to have the bedrooms they'd helped decorate for Penelope.

Vivian, on the other hand, wasn't sure she was ready to move on—again.

For nearly eight of the ten years she'd been married to Adam she'd lived in the small rundown house on the outskirts of town. But that ended when a late summer tornado blew the overgrown tree into the house. Still, she couldn't be more grateful that no one was home.

She and her girls were safe and living in a borrowed townhouse. But it was time to move on again.

It would be another three weeks or so before the other bedroom would be done so she could live in it. The contractor couldn't work until all of the daycare kids were gone for the day. For now, it looked like she and the two girls would be huddled up together. But that was okay. They were her strength and her sanity.

When they pulled up in front of the old house with the *Our Little Ones Daycare* sign out front, Penelope was standing on the porch with her hands on her oversized stomach.

BERNADETTE MARIE

The girls squealed to be let out of their seats, which Vivian did as quickly as she could. Both girls ran to Penelope, which tugged at Vivian's heart in a few different ways.

They loved Penelope. She was, she supposed, like an aunt to them. An aunt who happened to be carrying their sister or brother. A lump formed in her throat. Adam's baby.

Vivian opened the back of the car and began to tear out the suitcases. She thought she had a grasp on her feelings. But no. Clayton had to begin to ask questions and stir things up in her that she didn't want to admit were there.

She'd suppressed them so much she didn't realize she was angry or hurt as much as she was. She was mad, sure. Adam Monroe had screwed her over. He hadn't taken seriously the vows they took or the plans they'd made. He took two more wives and was having a baby with another woman.

She thought better of it as she threw another case out of the car and onto the ground. *He* wasn't having a baby with another woman—no—*she* was having a baby with Penelope.

It had become her responsibility and not his.

And the flood of tears broke and she didn't want that.

She looked around to see that no one was there, then she leaned against the car and wiped away her sadness.

Penelope wasn't her responsibility. All three of Adam's wives had chosen to stay where they were and work together. She could have left. She could stay angry. But she didn't want that.

The vibrant noise of children's laughter came from behind the house. But there were more giggles and laughs than her daughters.

She grabbed a suitcase in each hand and walked up the front walk and steps into the house.

Penelope fussed in the toddler room. It seemed to be something that calmed her, Vivian thought.

VIVIAN

"Are the girls out back?"

Penelope nodded with a delightful smile. "With Stephanie and Charlotte."

She could feel the blood drain from her head. "Clayton is here?"

Penelope shook her head and blonde curls bounced around her rosy cheeks. "He went with Brock to get some supplies to work on the bedroom."

"Why? I thought we had a guy doing that."

"It fell through. Brock and Clayton are going to do it."

Vivian tried to control her breath, her anger, her sadness—her lust.

Why did this man just keep coming back around? She didn't need his meddling into her life.

She carried the cases to the bedroom upstairs and set them down. Her mind cleared. Clayton North was a decent man that was all. Had she forgotten that they existed?

He was entrusting his angels in their care. She understood that he'd want to know they were taken care of. What better way to do that than to get to know the people taking care of them—personally?

As she set the cases on the bed, her mind wandered back to their conversation the night before. She'd been prepared for him to take his daughters and leave. Instead, his daughters were there, running with her daughters, and he wasn't there—at the moment.

Vivian sat down on the bed and let the air in her lungs whoosh out of her. He trusted them. Forget what Adam Monroe had done to all of them or what his mother threatened to do. Forget that someone had broken into the house a few weeks ago. He trusted.

Dear Lord, what could she accomplish if she had just a little bit of that trust?

Voices echoed up the stairs. Vivian rose from the bed, wiped her eyes, and sucked in some courage. In that moment of clarity, she knew she needed a friend like Clayton North in her life. Married or not, the man was opening her eyes to the world around her. It was time she took life by storm. No more hiding in rundown houses and bowing down to evil mother-in-laws. No more feeling bad that her husband thought so little of her. It was time for Vivian Monroe to take charge of her life and she owed that to the man who now stood outside the bedroom door smiling at her.

"Good morning," he said in a tone that brought fresh air into her lungs. "Did you sleep well last night?"

Vivian smiled—genuinely smiled. "No. I tossed and turned all night long. I couldn't sleep at all."

Clayton gave her a slow nod of consideration. "You seem very chipper for not getting any sleep."

She did, didn't she? "Just had an *ah-ha* moment. I guess I'm feeling good."

"Want to share?"

Vivian thought she just might want to until she saw Brock moving about in the bedroom across the hall. "I do. Maybe later."

Clayton flashed that sexy grin that usually made her insides turn to goo. Today, however, it filled her with warmth. She liked that.

"Maybe you can share with me over dinner. You did say you'd go with us for pizza tonight."

Vivian sucked in more of that courageous air. "You're right. I did. You offered up a family night. I look forward to spending time with your family," she said and then walked out of the room and down the stairs to gather more of her belongings.

VIVIAN

Clayton watched her disappear. She was a mystery, this one.

When he turned back into the other bedroom, Brock was sizing up the room. His hands were on his hips and his head nodded as though he were having a conversation in his head.

"What are you thinking?" Clayton set down the bag from the hardware store.

"That closet goes right up into the attic. What if we opened it up? It could almost be like a loft. Their own living room."

"Why not just use the steps in the hallway?"

"Well, because they're dangerous. They hit Sam in the chest and missed me by inches. Besides, it's closed up that way. If we open this up it would be roomy. Airy."

"And cold."

Brock smiled and held up a finger. "It needs insulation. Probably a new window too. I think I'll talk to Vivian and see what she thinks."

"You can do all that?"

Brock shrugged. "I don't know if I can do it all, but my dad and my brother sure can."

"They'd do that for her?"

"Of course," his brows narrowed. "That's what family does. They'll be here in a few weeks when the baby is born. I'll call him tonight and see what he thinks."

"They seemed to have really taken to Penelope. Your family that is."

Brock smiled. "Yeah, what's not to like about her though? She's perfect."

It was evident that this man standing in front of him was smitten and one hundred percent in love. It was nice to see. A man who came from a solid background and could show love. That in itself was a gift.

Clayton heard steps coming back up the stairs and when he looked out Vivian had her hands loaded down with more boxes and suitcases. He hurried out to take some of the load.

"I got this one," he said trying to relieve her arms of one of the boxes.

"I had it."

"I can help."

She dropped the items on the bed. "Why is that? Why are you always around to help?"

"I think I said yesterday, that's what friends do."

"Right. You said that. But it's a little freaky how you're always right where I need you."

"Freaky? I'd say it's lucky."

"Hmmm," she let out a grunt as her cell phone buzzed in her pocket. She quickly pulled it out and looked down at the text message that had arrived.

Clayton watched her read it, assumingly over and over again. Her cheeks had grown red and her jaw twitched, she was clenching it so tightly.

"Everything okay?"

Her eyes moved back to his. They'd grown dark—and angry.

"Everything is fine. I don't need you to pick up the pieces of everything. You can't fix everything. I don't even know you."

She shoved her phone back in her pocket and walked out of the room.

Clayton tucked his hands in his pockets and took a moment to relax. She really did need some help to get through all of this.

Vivian's hands shook. She was hiding in the bathroom downstairs just watching them shake.

VIVIAN

She looked down at the text message one more time. *I haven't forgotten about you.*

Sweat beaded on her brow. With the back of her hand, she wiped it off and looked into the mirror. Maybe they weren't safe there anymore.

The text had come from Adam's mother's phone. Just as the text had the night someone had broken into the old house.

She was going to have to tell Amelia about this. Penelope was too fragile right now. But, damn, she thought. She was going to need to tell Clayton too and he was going to have to pull the girls' enrollment.

There was a knock at the door. "I have to go potty," a small voice called.

Vivian pulled herself together and opened the door. Emma rushed past her and into the bathroom. She let her have her privacy, but she stood just beyond the door. What about the girls? Her girls weren't safe anymore.

Chapter Four

Could they fit more video games into a small pizza parlor? Clayton was happy, though, to see that there was an old Ms PacMan game in the corner.

He sat at a table for six, but so far only he and his girls had arrived. He was beginning to wonder if Vivian had changed her mind.

"I'm hungry. Do we have to wait?" Stephanie whined.

"Go ahead. If we don't eat, it's going to get cold." He dished out a slice of cheese pizza to each of the girls and then watched the door, just as he'd been doing for a half hour already.

After forty-five minutes, Clayton finally had a slice of cold cheese pizza.

It was obvious that things weren't going the way he'd hoped they would with Vivian. It was quite obvious she was blind to the fact that he was interested. Okay, he could handle that. He hadn't come to Parson's Gulch to find a woman. In fact, that had never crossed his mind. He didn't want another woman—ever. Or that's what he'd kept telling himself. But then he'd met her.

Vivian Monroe, the woman with the dark mesmerizing eyes and silky chocolate hair—and a chip on her shoulder the size of a boulder.

It would forever be obvious they both needed their healing space. He wasn't healed yet, and, he figured that's why he was tossing his heart around.

He rubbed at the back of his neck. If he wasn't healed yet then why try to heal someone else? Wasn't that just a bad combination?

Clayton knew he certainly didn't need any more drama in his life. His girls didn't need it either. Maybe it was good they hadn't shown up. This gave him a clear view of what he was doing and it wasn't in the best interest of everyone.

Vivian Monroe was a strong woman who didn't want anyone's help. She wanted to keep everything hidden away and let it stew—let it burn. Fine. There was always the rec center. Clayton didn't *have* to leave the girls with them next week, though he liked their set-up. He liked Penelope's gentle touch with Charlotte. Damn—he was simply too far into it now. He didn't want to give up on Vivian.

"Daddy, look!" Charlotte nearly bounced out of her booster seat to point toward the door.

When he turned back around, he saw two grinning faces running toward them. Emma and Ava scooted into the booth and instantly began making young conversation with their friends.

"Where's your mommy?" he asked, having never seen her.

"She told us to sit here. She's ordering a pizza."

That wasn't the plan. He stood from his seat but could only see the top of her head over the small wall. He certainly couldn't leave four talkative toddlers sitting at the table alone.

A moment later she came around the wall. A weight was on her shoulders. And though she was smiling at him, he could see something was wrong.

"I'm very sorry we were late. I was in Sam's office and…" she closed her eyes and let out a breath before opening them again. "I'm sorry."

"No need. I have pizza." He pointed down to the pieces of congealed cheese.

VIVIAN

"I knew I'd ruined your plans. A hot one is coming. You can heat that up for lunch tomorrow. School lunches are never very good."

He laughed. "You're right. They aren't. Have a seat."

She sat on the edge of the circular booth and he on the other end. Four chatty little girls sat between them talking Disney Princesses and My Little Ponies. Vivian, on the other hand, watched the door.

How was he going to get this woman alone so they could talk? They needed to talk. She needed to talk.

"Ball pit, Daddy. We want to go in the ball pit," Stephanie took over the planning of the evening.

"Why don't you take all of them? I'll wait for the pizza."

It wasn't quite what he wanted to do, but he would. However, he'd be watching her very closely.

Clayton nodded and followed four little girls to the small ball pit in the corner, which he was sure was filled with nothing but germs that would have to be bathed off of them.

Vivian glanced at the door and then toward the kitchen where she knew there was a back door. She'd been at Sam's office all afternoon, just as she'd told Clayton she had been. They'd pulled in Darby, the officer who had been called when the house had been broken into a few weeks before.

The break-in had been written off as a string of vandalism crimes that had happened that night. But Vivian had always known better. Someone had been in that attic looking for the money Adam's grandmother had hid in all the vintage books. But now—now the text had her frightened. She was sincerely considering a bigger move than one to the house on Main and Pine. Maybe it was time to just disappear off the map.

It would mean leaving Penelope and Amelia with all Adam's crap. But if it meant security for her and the girls—well that's all she could think about now.

Vivian looked at the table. There were only three glasses. Hadn't he said it was a family dinner night? Where was his wife? Certainly she would have come for dinner.

A young girl delivered the pizza to the table. Vivian thanked her, and though her stomach growled in anticipation of tasting hot food, she walked across the restaurant to the ball pit.

The familiar giggle and screeches of the four girls was music to her ears. It would devastate her girls if she moved them away from Clayton's girls.

"You look preoccupied," Clayton said.

She looked up and he was looking down at her with brown eyes that could easily wrap her in the comfort she was craving. "I suppose I am. No worries."

He shifted his glance back to the girls. "They are going to need a bath. It makes my skin crawl just thinking about what's in that ball pit."

"Just like life, right? The worst things are the most fun?"

The comment had made him laugh and he had an easy, sexy laugh. Vivian fisted her hands to her side. She was pathetic. He was her ball pit. Everything about him said it would be a bad thing to keep showing up places with him while he wore that ring on his finger, but he made her feel good.

"Why don't we go back to my house?" he offered. "We can get those girls cleaned up, they can watch a movie, and we could eat some pizza without all this noise."

Vivian felt it coming on—the desire to go to his home, the aching need to talk to someone who wasn't married to Adam Monroe or knew him. And yet that stupid gold band—

and absence of a wife—was confusing her until her stomach was in such a knot she thought she might get sick right there.

"Why are you asking me to your house?"

Clayton dropped his shoulders. "Because this place is giving me a headache. I'd love to sit and actually talk to you." He turned and faced her, shoving his hands into his pockets. "You don't trust me do you?"

"I don't know you."

"Oh, I think we've established that quite a few times."

She could feel that prickling anger creep up her spine. "Listen, I don't know what your situation is, but I'm no home wrecker. I married one of those and I don't need any more of it in my life. So, if you have other plans then I have to tell you I'm not…"

He held up his hand and closed his eyes as if he were mentally willing her to stop talking—so she did.

"Whoa." He opened his eyes and they flared temper. "Who in the world would accuse you of being a home wrecker?"

"Anyone who saw me having dinner with you and if they see me going home with you. Oh, and then there is the fact that you've been at my house all week."

Now his eyes narrowed and he took a step toward her. "Friends. Are you telling me people in this town don't understand friendships?"

"Sure. Just not between a newly widowed woman and a married man."

"Married? And wait, what about Amelia and Penelope? They are both engaged and newly widowed."

"And no one knows they were Adam's wives but you."

"Oh, I see since I'm a good enough friend to know all your secrets, but I'm not a good enough friend to have you over?"

"I just don't understand why you…"

Her voice had risen, but she hadn't noticed until Stephanie and Emma were standing in front of them.

Emma tugged on her shirt. "Are you mad at Stephanie's dad?"

Vivian looked at her and then at Stephanie whose eyes were equally as sad and confused as her own daughter's.

Clayton reached his hand to Emma's shoulder. "Your mom and I just need to talk away from all this noise. I was thinking you all could come to our house for just a little bit."

"Yes!" Both girls answered simultaneously.

"Go get the others."

They ran toward the ball pit.

Vivian fisted her hands on her hips. "That wasn't fair."

"Looks like it's the only way I can talk to you. You seem to have some preconceived ideas brewing in your head."

She clenched her teeth. "I don't like to be tricked."

"I was pretty open with the invitation." He watched the girls bring back their sisters. "One hour. I want one hour of your time."

He turned and walked the girls back to the table.

Fine. She'd give him one hour. What did he need her for? Why did she feel the need to follow him?

She watched him with the four young girls as they gathered jackets and items they'd carried in. He was amazing with them and she assumed he was equally as amazing when he was in a classroom.

As he joked with them and they giggled, she saw a light in her girls' eyes she hadn't seen in awhile. It tugged at her heart.

When he turned to her and those brown eyes were soft and inviting that goo began to puddle in her belly again. Then the corner of his mouth turned up and her heart lodged in her throat. Only once had a man smiled at her like that and

VIVIAN

the world stopped. But it was happening again, only this time she was much older and so much wiser.

However, when he gave a nod toward the door, she couldn't help it. She followed like the lost puppy she was. There was a deep urge to get to spend this forbidden hour with him at his house. She was going to hell for this.

Chapter Five

It wasn't until the moment they walked in the door that Clayton remembered the sink full of dishes. He winced.

At least he'd taken a moment during the day to tidy up the living room and the bathroom was clean.

As Vivian and her girls pulled up, Stephanie and Charlotte began their assault on his ears. But as he watched them jump up and down as Vivian unbuckled Emma and Ava it brought a certain joy to him. They loved those girls and that excitement was contagious.

The moment Emma and Ava ran through the door, the four of them were off to the bedroom where he could already hear talk of the many fairy tale items strewn all over the floor.

Vivian walked toward the door, her arms full of jackets, holding the box of pizza from the restaurant. "They forget when the sun goes down it gets cold."

"I forget that too," he joked as he stepped aside and let her into the house.

There was always that uncomfortable moment when someone walked into his house and looked around.

"The girls are all in the bedroom comparing toys."

She nodded. "I'm sure my girls are loving that. Most of their toys were destroyed in the tornado."

There was an immediate reaction that spiked inside of him and he reached a hand out to her shoulder. "Your house was destroyed in that tornado?"

"The old tree out front blew into the house. So it wasn't hit by the tornado, but damage was done."

He cupped her shoulder in his hand and left it there. "I'm so sorry."

VIVIAN

"Don't be. It was a horrible little house full of bad memories. Sam made sure we had a place to live."

He let his hand fall from her shoulder and brush down her arm. "He's a good man."

"The best." She looked around again. "Can I set these somewhere?"

"Oh, yes." He shut the front door and took the jackets from her. "I'll set them here." He placed them on a chair in the corner where he would usually sit and read while the girls watched TV. "Please excuse the mess too. I've been busy with my classroom, not my house."

"Don't apologize on my behalf."

He wasn't very good at entertaining. "I'm going to make a pot of coffee. I'll take the pizza and put it in the refrigerator. Unless you want a slice now."

She shook her head. "I'm not really hungry and it looks like the girls are otherwise occupied at the moment."

He took the box from her. "Make yourself at home."

Vivian watched him hurry away. It wasn't very often she made someone so nervous.

The term *make yourself at home* was always odd to her. The house was small and old. It would need a lot of updating over the next year, but it was cozy, she thought.

The shelf where the TV sat looked to be a handmade shelf. It had detailed carvings running down it and was beautifully stained.

She couldn't help but be drawn to it and run her fingers down the carvings. As she did her eyes drew to the photos on the shelves. A mass of pictures of Stephanie and Charlotte over the past few years stared back at her. But what she noticed was they were all photos with a woman—Linda.

Vivian's heart stalled with a giant kick that physically hurt. None of the pictures of Charlotte were current. In the center of all the frames was a family photo. Clayton with his arm wrapped around Linda, Stephanie on his hip and Charlotte in Linda's arms, perhaps only a few months old.

She couldn't help but want to touch it.

"I didn't know if you liked cream." His voice carried through the room, but there was deep sadness in it.

She turned to see him in the doorway watching her. "Is this Linda?"

He tucked his lips between his teeth as he walked toward her. Handing her the mug of coffee, he nodded.

A faint smile formed on his lips. "Yeah, that's her. Beautiful, isn't she?"

Vivian swallowed hard and looked at the woman with the firm, athletic build. Blonde hair cascaded down her shoulders and her smile was bright.

"She is. You have a beautiful family."

He nodded still looking at the picture. "Charlotte might have been three months old. We were hiking in the Colorado Rocky Mountains. What a view."

Still, his voice hadn't returned to normal. Now it actually shook when he talked. It was at that moment she realized there was a reason Linda hadn't been there for dinner.

Noting the sadness that filled his eyes and his voice, Vivian raised her hand to his arm, just as he'd done to her the night before.

"Where is she?"

"Seattle," he said flatly as he continued to stare at the photo, but now his eyes grew moist.

It really wasn't what she thought he'd say.

"Seattle? Why didn't she move with you?"

VIVIAN

Finally, he turned, his eyes brimming with tears. "She's buried in Seattle."

Her heart exploded in her chest and she felt her own tears burning in her throat and then her eyes. It didn't take but a breath and a sorrowful look from Clayton to have them spilling down her cheeks.

"Oh, Clayton." She wanted to brush away her tears, but she couldn't remove her hand from his arm. She wanted to touch him.

"C'mon, now." He cleared his throat. "We're in the same boat here. I can't let you get all emotional about my loss."

She looked around the room and saw the small coffee table behind her. She set her mug down and turned back to him. Then she moved to him and pulled him in. Wrapping her arms around his neck, she stood on her toes and held on. Her head rested on his shoulder, but he was stiff beneath her. But she wasn't going to let go.

A moment later she could feel his body quiver beneath hers and his arms came around her, one hand still holding a cup of coffee.

He was crying against her hair and she was sobbing into his shoulder.

They were both broken and they held each other tighter. They were both wounded and they each cried a little harder.

"Daddy." A soft, faint voice said behind them.

Vivian slowly pulled back and Clayton wiped frantically at his eyes.

"Hey, baby."

"Why you cry?" Charlotte asked and it broke through Vivian's hard exterior and she had to turn from the little girl to wipe away her tears.

"Just missing mommy."

Vivian turned to see the girl simply nod her head. This was an obviously normal reaction to her seeing him cry. Yet the young girl didn't cry.

"*Frozen.*"

Clayton chuckled. "I'll put it on TV. Go get the girls and you can all watch out here. Vivian and I will go talk in the kitchen."

Charlotte nodded and ran to the bedroom.

"I'll take our coffee in there," Vivian offered and with a nod he handed her his mug.

She walked back to the kitchen where she stopped, noticing the sink full of dishes. That wouldn't do for this man. He needed some help.

Vivian set the mugs down on the small table in the corner and moved toward the sink where she began to arrange the dishes onto the counter.

Logically she looked under the sink for the dish soap, where she found it, and filled the sink with suds.

"You're going to do my dishes because I made you cry?"

She turned to look at him. He was leaned against the doorway watching her. So relaxed. So sexy. She could simply eat him but, but he was broken too. That she needed to remember.

He'd said they were in the same boat, but really, they weren't.

She'd lost Adam years ago. The fact that she'd even gotten pregnant with Ava was a miracle. She and Adam had pounced on each other one time that trip. Hormones had raged, sex had happened, then the fights started and he'd left.

But Clayton still wore his ring.

Their situation was nothing alike.

VIVIAN

"I'm going to do your dishes because I'm a little emotional right now. I need to occupy myself and you could use some help."

"I don't need help," he said, but when she looked at him, he was smiling again.

"Let me. I'm going to explode if I don't do this."

His eyes were locked on hers and he moved to her. "I know how you feel."

"You do?"

He rested his hand on her arm and turned her to face him directly. Then both hands were on her arms and she was gazing up into his still moist, reddened eyes.

"How did Adam die?"

Really? He was standing two inches from her, holding her arms like that and he wanted to know about Adam?

"Landmine," she choked out the words. "He saved Brock then led them out of harm and into a mine field."

Clayton nodded. "Brave man."

The tears were back and her body just wanted to fall to the floor and curl up in a ball.

"Yes. He was brave."

A tear rolled over her cheek and Clayton raised his hand to brush it away with his thumb.

He bit down on his lip, slid his hands down her arms until their hands clasped together. His eyes locked in again with hers.

"Fourteen year old boy was distraught by his parents' divorce. He'd begun acting up in class, but Linda took him under her wing. She helped him with homework and talked to him for hours about how he felt about what was happening at home. She'd had Charlotte in May, took off the last month of school and went back to work in September. It had given the boy all summer to stew over this crush he had on his teacher. On Linda."

Vivian's hands began to clench around Clayton's. He wasn't looking into her eyes anymore. He was looking down between them at their hands clasped together as if they were both holding on for dear life.

"October second he decided that he was mad enough that he took a gun to school."

Vivian held her breath.

"He shot the secretary who stopped him from going into the school because he'd been expelled due to threats. She survived. He shot a girl who happened to be kissing a boy in the corner because it angered him. She survived. The boy went after him, he shot him. The boy died."

Vivian gasped for breath and held it too.

"Linda had her class locked in the room. He was prepared for that. Somehow he'd broken the lock to her room prior to his entering that day. All it took was a kick with his foot. Linda stepped in front of her students to protect them. He shot her, then shot himself."

The breath came now and so did the tears. They rolled down her cheeks and straight to the floor. Their hands stayed firmly clasped together, her fingers numb, but not letting go.

"He survived. She died."

Chapter Six

Never had Clayton told that story to someone. Either people knew it or they didn't. And never did he want to tell it again.

His heart was racing so fast he thought he'd better sit down and breathe, but he couldn't. He couldn't let go of Vivian's hands.

Her tears rolled off her cheeks and had puddled between them on the floor. The beautiful lips that would smile at him were swollen and red, and so was the tip of her nose.

"I moved here to separate the girls from it. He was a juvenile. He won't be in prison forever."

"You seem so strong. How are you so strong?"

Clayton shook his head. "I'm not. Strong would be staying in Seattle where our families were. Strong would be visiting her grave every day. I ran. I ran to escape it so I didn't have to see it every day when I drove down the street. I ran so no one would look at me and think *you poor man*."

"You needed to run. What else would you have done?"

"For a month I drank. Another month I exercised until they nearly hospitalized me. Then I got help."

Her head rose and her eyes seared into his. "What does that mean?"

"It means I think you need help too. And if there is a God or there is fate, I think this is the path I was meant to be on. A path right to you."

Now she let go. "Don't say you're here to save me."

"That's not what I meant." He raked his numb fingers through his hair. "I've had two years to let this eat at me. I asked for help. I got it. I asked for help for the girls. They got it. I felt as though I'd gotten enough help that I could move

VIVIAN

on—move away. Your wounds are still fresh, Vivian. You haven't faced it all yet. I want to be here for you."

"You're talking crazy now." She wiped her eyes and turned back toward his sink of dishes and soapy water.

It all burned in him now. Linda's loss. Adam's loss. Vivian's defiance. And that urge to move on.

He took her arm and spun her toward him until their bodies were pressed together. He expected her to fight him— slug him even. But she didn't

Clayton cupped the back of her neck in his hand. Her lips parted as he looked down at her. He had to remind himself it was okay to move on. Both of them could move on.

Closing his eyes, he lowered his mouth to hers and took control of moving on.

It ached in Vivian's head, her chest, all the way to her toes—the need. His mouth was on hers and she opened to his kiss—warm and inviting.

Her back was against the wet counter, but who would care, when a man could make your head spin as Clayton was doing to her.

The hand at the back of her neck slid up into her hair and his other hand came to her waist.

It had been a long time since a man held her like this. His body pressed to hers so firmly she could feel the heat from his skin through layers of clothes. The taste of coffee on his lips and the explosion when his tongue pressed to find hers was enough to get drunk on.

Vivian raised her hands to his chest and his heart hammered against her fingertips. He deepened the kiss even further and her breath was a moan against his mouth.

She lifted her arms around his neck and hung on for dear life, as her heart began to beat in erratic rhythm with his and then began to tumble, somewhere she never thought it would tumble again—in love.

When his lips left hers, they skimmed across her jaw line to her ear where she caught the sound of his moan and breath. She pulled him in tighter.

His lips then traveled down her neck to the crevice of her collarbone and a lightning bolt of nearly orgasmic pleasure ripped through her.

Her fingers now dug at the collar of his shirt. It was hard to breathe they were pressed so hard together, but every moment had an ending. This one ended when a loud thunder of "Let it go!" came from the living room as all four girls sang with the movie.

Vivian felt his body jolt in a chuckle as he nuzzled his face into her neck.

"Impeccable timing," he breathed the words into her ear, but he didn't let go of her.

"Is this smart of us?"

He pressed his forehead to hers. "I'm very lousy with giving hints." He nipped her lips with a kiss. "I've been interested in you since the minute I came to the door looking for daycare."

"I've never talked so fast in my life," she laughed remembering the day she'd become some smitten little girl.

"You blew me off at the barbecue."

"You wear a wedding ring."

And then, as if he'd forgotten all about it, he moved his hand so he could see it. "So I do."

"I wasn't going to wreck your home."

He brushed his fingers through her hair. "I'm fairly sure you just helped me build a new one.

~*~

60

VIVIAN

Vivian stared at the ceiling of her bedroom. It had been nearly eleven o'clock when they'd left Clayton's house. Now it was well past one o'clock and she couldn't sleep at all.

Her body still buzzed. Her skin was still warm. Her heart felt full.

It had taken her a few hours to realize what it was that she really felt—she was happy.

She'd expected that the girls would have to be pulled from his house, but it had been her. They'd sat down with the girls to finish watching the movie—because they simply couldn't trust themselves alone.

As soon as they'd sat down on the couch both sets of girls had climbed up and joined them. Clayton had draped his arm across the back of the couch and laid his fingertips on the back of her neck.

Even in her bed—alone—she could still feel his touch on her skin.

All four girls had fallen asleep piled on them. As the movie played the credits she and Clayton had simply sat there gazing at each other. The girls slept between them.

It would have been so simple to let the girls sleep, to sneak away, and sleep in his arms. But they both knew that wasn't going to work.

She closed her eyes. They'd both been broken. What if it wasn't real, these feelings they were having. What if they broke each other more?

Vivian rolled to her side, rearranged her pillow, and tried to get comfortable.

She couldn't have been asleep more than a few moments when she heard the pitter-patter of little feet and a small hand reached up and touched her arm.

"Mommy, I sleep here?"

She pried open her eyes to see Ava standing there looking up at her, Emma standing behind her.

"Girls, what's the matter?"

"We miss you."

She weakly smiled at them and scooted over in the bed to make room for them. After a few moments of them bouncing and adjusting in the bed, she closed her eyes.

"Mommy."

Vivian opened one eye and looked at Emma.

"Stephanie and Charlotte's mommy died."

"Yes, baby."

"Our daddy died," Ava added.

"Yes he did, baby."

The girls looked at each other and Vivian propped herself up on her elbow. Had it finally hit home after all these months? He hadn't been around much. The girls didn't really know him, especially Ava.

"We all thought if you married their daddy we could be a family."

The words squeezed at her heart. "We are a family. The three of us. And we have Amelia and Sam. Penelope and Brock are our family too."

"And the baby," Ava yawned.

"And the baby."

Emma sat up in the bed. "But they need a mommy and we need a daddy. And then we'd be sisters."

She had quite a grasp on the situation, Vivian thought.

"I just met their daddy. I think we are a long way from making plans like that."

Emma thought for a moment. "But Brock and Penelope just met."

She was grasping much more than she'd ever have given her credit for.

VIVIAN

"Go to sleep. We can talk about this later. I'm not getting married any time soon. But I wouldn't mind spending more time with Clayton and his girls."

Emma nodded. That seemed to suffice all the curiosity from her daughter.

Vivian closed her eyes again and smiled in the dark. They wanted a daddy. In the past six months, she'd seen that stranger things could happen—even she could get a man who was interested.

Because they'd fallen asleep at Clayton's, Vivian's girls must have gotten much more sleep than she had. She was exhausted.

The girls were plopped down in front of the TV watching a movie while she watched the pot of coffee brew.

It had been decided she and the girls would move to the old house on Main and Pine. Brock and Clayton had already purchased paint and made plans for the bedroom.

She closed her eyes and breathed in the moment. He'd had eyes for her since the moment he'd knocked on the door.

Her heart fluttered in her chest. She opened her eyes, took down a coffee mug, and waited.

The kiss he'd planted on her had rocked her. Every nerve in her body still sparked and when she even thought about the kiss—she grew warm.

They didn't have plans to see each other today, but she couldn't help but hope that something would come up and he'd come by. After all, she had to pack up the few things they still possessed after the tornado. He always seemed to show up when she needed him.

A surge passed through her and she let out a near moan—she certainly needed him.

Chapter Seven

Charlotte had woken up early and now was taking a nap. Stephanie had asked to watch "*Frozen*" again, and to keep her quiet Clayton had let her.

But as he cleaned his kitchen and swapped out laundry, he really wanted to be with Vivian.

A half hour later, Charlotte woke up crying and Stephanie was now asleep on the couch. At what point would he even get them out of the house for some sun?

As he carried the laundry basket to the bedroom, he noticed the papers on his desk. With a grunt, he gave up all hope of kissing the woman who had made him feel whole again—even if only for a few moments. He had lesson plans to finish and papers to grade. It didn't look like he was going to be able to just drop by and see her as he'd planned.

Setting the basket on his bed, he took out the first dress and set it into Charlotte's pile and repeated the process. When his phone rang, he nearly jumped over the bed to grab it off the nightstand. Everything in him surged to life and he hoped Vivian was on the other end of the line.

He slid his finger over the screen, "Hello." His voice had even sounded chipper. When was the last time that had happened?

"Clayton," the woman's voice on the other end said softly.

That surge of life, which had bubbled inside of him when the phone range, sizzled away.

"Dorothy." His voice dropped and his heart squeezed until it hurt. "How are you?"

Linda's mother let out a dreadful sigh, which had Clayton sitting down on the bed.

VIVIAN

"Good days. Bad days."

He understood that well enough. Up until she'd called, it had been one of his good days.

Dorothy let out another noise—a groan. "How are my granddaughters? I miss them so much."

The pain in his chest intensified. "They're doing well. They start in a new daycare center tomorrow."

"That's wonderful. Are they making friends?"

That made him smile. "As a matter of fact, they are. The woman with the daycare center has girls the same ages as mine. They have quickly become best friends."

"That makes me happy." Her voice had risen and he knew she needed to know that. "How about you? Are you doing okay?"

She'd always been considerate of him. He appreciated that. "I am. The new job is going well."

"And friends. Have you made any new friends?"

When she mentioned it, the flutters of life moved inside of him again. "I have made some good friends. A few couples and a woman who lost her husband in June."

"Oh, Clayton. There is too much of this going on."

"Hers died in combat."

"God bless him." She was silent for a few moments. "Will you bring the girls home for Christmas? I know we would all love to see them. We miss you all so much."

Clayton hadn't much thought about it. He should go back for Christmas. He'd moved from Seattle to mend himself, but he knew it had only made things worse for everyone else.

"I'll consider it."

"I hope you will. Will you have the girls call me on Tuesday night? We got that Skype stuff figured out on my computer. I can't wait to see the girls again."

It brought a smile to his face when he remembered Skyping with her the first time "I'll make sure we do. The girls will love to see you."

She said her goodbyes and Clayton disconnected the call. He felt the lead ball of guilt dropping in his stomach. He sat down on the bed and fell back. Laundry—or anything else—didn't seem so important now.

Moving away from Seattle was supposed to make him move on. But he missed Linda every day—or he had until this morning when he woke and she wasn't the very first thing on his mind. Vivian had taken that place this morning.

~*~

Sam had called and let Vivian know that the man who had lent them the townhouse had a renter. It was official. She had four days to get out. Luckily they had nothing and Penelope was all moved out of the old house. She just wished all the bedrooms had been finished.

Really, why did she care? It was still nicer than the house she lived in that she and Adam had bought.

Every box she packed she set by the front door and checked her phone for the time. The entire day had passed and Clayton hadn't called, texted, or dropped by.

Every time she checked the time, a part of her heart began to harden. It had been a mistake that kiss Clayton had planted on her. It had been wrong to inhale it, hold it, to want it. She should have socked him in the gut.

But she hadn't, so now she was nursing a broken heart.

It was nearly six o'clock when Emma tugged on her shirt. "Are we having dinner?"

The question only added to her heartbreak. She'd neglected her children all day as she'd packed. She'd thrown together some peanut butter and jelly sandwiches for lunch. Cut up an apple for snack. They'd watched movies, packed up their toys, and stayed out of her way. It wasn't that she was too busy—they didn't have very many possessions. She was just preoccupied in thought—about Clayton.

"I'm sorry, sweetheart. Why don't we drive over to McDonald's? I'll buy you a Happy Meal since you've been so patient with me today."

Emma's eyes opened wide and she immediately ran to collect her sister. Vivian decided that might have been the only thing that had made her smile all day.

They were on the road in less than five minutes. She thought it was funny how easily you could bribe children with junk food. She was smart to save the bribe though. She figured her kids had only had maybe three Happy Meals ever. Yes, it was better kept for a treat.

Once their order was placed they found a table near the play yard. She'd remembered how Clayton had reacted to the ball pit at the pizza restaurant. She wondered how he'd react to something like a playground like this.

"I guess we parent alike."

Vivian looked up at the voice that had been in her head all day. Her mouth was full of hamburger, so all she could do was swallow hard when she saw Clayton standing above her with a tray of food.

"What are you guys doing here?"

He set the tray down at the table next to them as the girls went about gabbing as if they hadn't seen each other less than twenty-four hours ago.

"I'm bribing kids. They've never had a Happy Meal and I wasn't in the mood to cook. Though I now have clean dishes, thank you."

"They've never had a Happy Meal?"

He shook his head as he handed each girl her box. "No. Linda was very specific about it. I would have let them junk out a few times, but it wasn't part of her parenting model."

"And you've stuck to it?"

"It was one of the best ways I could honor her."

She couldn't help but notice his voice dragged when he spoke and his eyes were sad. Suddenly she wondered what might have happened.

He sat next to her on the bench, though at the other table with his girls. In what seemed like a quick moment, the girls were done and had run off to play in the play yard, leaving only trash and half eaten hamburgers in their wake.

Clayton's hunched shoulders and quiet mannerism had her worried. She wasn't one to not stick her nose into things. However, now wasn't the time to start sitting back and being quiet.

"Is everything okay? You look upset."

He lifted his head and looked at her. With a forced smile, he slid across the booth until he was seated next to her.

Even though he looked miserable, just having him sitting right next to her made her body buzz just as it had last night.

"I got a phone call this morning from Linda's mom."

"Oh," she said as she felt her own mood sink.

"She misses the girls and wants to see them."

"Of course she does."

Clayton ran his hands over his hair. "I needed to get away from it all. Two years among it nearly drove me mad. But I hurt everyone when I left."

"You can't feel guilty."

"Oh, yes I can," he said reaching for her hand and holding it in his.

It seemed so natural and suddenly she wanted to cry. He needed comfort—from her.

68

VIVIAN

"Are you considering moving back?" She had to ask, but she wasn't sure she wanted the answer.

"The thought crossed my mind about ten minutes after I moved here. But then I met you and the girls met your girls. I feel as though I've become friends with Sam and Brock and, well," he finally smiled. "I feel like I belong here."

That was more of what she wanted to hear.

"Can I be honest? I thought maybe you regretted our kiss last night."

He turned and narrowed his gaze on her. "Why would you think that?"

"I've become accustomed to you just showing up when I need you. Even when I don't know that I need you."

He lifted his hand to her cheek and then brushed his fingers back into her hair. "I woke up this morning wanting to run over to your house. All it would have taken was to tell the girls we could go play and they'd have been in the car. But when Dorothy, Linda's mother," he explained. "When she called me and she sounded so broken, I just couldn't do anything but lay on my bed."

"You have a good relationship with her family?"

A faint smile crossed his lips. "Yes. I couldn't have asked for better in-laws."

Jealousy shot through her. Wouldn't that have been nice? She'd spent more time with Adam's parents over the past year than she had with her own. But it was never pleasant. She wouldn't have called them ideal. Even Frank was a bit moody. And Stella—well, what could she say that was nice? Nothing.

The sound of giggling caught their attention and they both turned their heads to see the girls standing inside the play structure looking at them. Their gazing into each other's eyes had set the four little girls into a fit of delighted giggles. When they'd looked at them, all four of them ducked.

Clayton shook his head. "We've been caught."

"Oh, if only they'd seen us last night." She felt the heat rise in her cheeks when she thought about it. "I enjoyed it, by the way. I want you to know."

"I did too."

Her mind wandered to the conversation she'd had with her girls in the middle of the night. "My girls thought we should get married so they could be sisters with your girls."

Clayton burst into laughter, which caught her off guard and became contagious. "Mine mentioned that. Do you think they saw us?"

"And moved from in front of the TV? No way."

He looked back at the play yard and saw a few sets of eyes peering through a round window in a colorful tube. "Should we make them scream?"

Vivian's eyes followed to where he'd been looking. "What did you have in mind?"

He didn't tell her his plan. Instead he leaned in and pressed a kiss to her lips. The squeals from the colorful tube ignited and Vivian's lips curled into a smile under Clayton's.

As he pulled back, he looked toward the girls. "I knew that would get them."

"What are they going to think?"

"That their parents are happy."

And she was. It had been a very long time since she had been.

"I have to work tomorrow," Clayton began.

"So do I," Vivian interrupted with a grin.

"Yes you do." He gave her hand a squeeze. "I was thinking, why don't you all come over for a little while? Not as late as last night of course."

VIVIAN

Vivian gave some thought. "Why don't you come to our house? I have a few more boxes to pack."

"Moving are you? Officially?"

"Yes. Sam got a call today that the owner has a renter."

"I guess we'd better get to working on that room for you. Brock has some grand plans."

"Does he? He'd better get busy on it. He's going to have his hands full soon."

"I think he'll make a good father."

That warmed her. "You know, I think he will too."

Chapter Eight

There was no reason for Vivian to think about apologizing for the state of her house. After all, he knew she was moving and she'd washed his sink full of dishes.

The thought made her chuckle as he walked through the front door.

With a grand sweeping look he said, "It's a shame to give up this place. It's nice."

"Thousand times better than the dump we lived in on the edge of town. But the old house will be nice too—for now."

The girls ran off to play with a warning from Clayton, "One hour. I have school tomorrow and you start the new daycare."

That was met with screams of anticipation rather than the grunts she'd expected on the hour time frame.

"And I still have lesson plans to write," he muttered.

"I thought you were going to do that today."

Clayton shrugged. "Dorothy's phone call kinda threw me off my game. Not kinda," he reconsidered. "It did. It's been a few weeks since I was immobile and unable to do anything."

Vivian realized she really hadn't had too many of those days. The ones she'd had weren't because Adam was gone. It was because he'd screwed her over.

"Can I get you something to drink? I don't have much. Maybe a glass of wine, a juice box, milk, or water."

"Is it too late for coffee?"

"Not if you have to do lesson plans," she teased as she walked toward the kitchen.

VIVIAN

On autopilot she went about making coffee—filling water, scooping coffee grounds, pulling down mugs. But when she turned he was right there.

His hands came to her hips and their bodies quickly pressed against each other. Clayton's mouth moved to hers swiftly and devoured her in a kiss that had her bracing against the counter to keep standing.

His hand moved from her hip to her cheek, and into her hair. The kiss grew deeper—hotter—until she released the counter and locked her arms around the man making her mind numb.

How could this man be so distraught over his wife and then kiss the strength out of her bones? And why was she letting him? There should be some common sense to step away until he'd recovered from what had happened to his wife, but she couldn't seem to make the step. Though just as quickly she thought about being just a replacement and she didn't want that either.

But damn, he tasted so good and her gooey insides were too enjoyable to not appreciate.

When his lips finally slipped from hers, his forehead remained pressed against hers.

"I would have much rather done that all day," he said, his voice low and thick.

This would be the perfect time to stall this relationship—or fling—they seemed to be starting. Okay, maybe just a good time to feel it out.

"Does it bother you to kiss me like this when you've been upset over your wife all day?"

Clayton stepped back from her and let his hands slide down to grasp hers. "I can't get her back. I can't dwell on what was taken from me. It hurts. It hurts so damn much there are days like today that I'm immobilized." He moved back toward her. "And then there are kisses like that that make me feel again. There is still a stirring in me to be part of something. I want to love again."

That was a warning to her and she slid away from beneath him and turned her attention to the coffee maker.

"I said something wrong." He moved toward the table and let out a deep breath.

"It's nothing. Really."

"It can't be nothing or you would have let me kiss you again."

Vivian took the pot of coffee and poured the mugs full. Setting the pot back on the warmer, she turned to face him.

"I've only ever been with Adam. And obviously that was a long time ago. I don't want to be the person someone uses to move on from a bad situation."

She saw a spark of something in his eyes. Was it anger? Regret?

"You think that's what I'm doing?"

"I don't know what you're doing. You just keep showing up and then we're kissing."

"You were kissing me too."

"I know." She let her shoulders drop and let the anger blow out of her lungs. "I know."

Clayton rubbed the whiskers on his cheeks. Obviously he'd been distraught enough he hadn't shaved, but Vivian couldn't help but think it had given him a sexy edge. Then again, here she was arguing with him over what they'd been doing—thinking he was sexy wasn't helping.

"I'm not here to just forget about my wife. I'll never forget her. I fell in love with her when I was sixteen years old. We had a good life. I'm bitter that someone took that away from me."

VIVIAN

And with those words she realized that was what she was. She was bitter that someone had taken her good life away from her—someone named Stella Monroe.

She had loved Adam and he had loved her. Had she not bought into Stella's lies about how she shouldn't travel with him and she should stay near his family, maybe he would have known how much she did love him.

They had a family together. Once they'd had a life together. How could she have been so blind for so long?

It gnawed at her that he'd wanted a divorce and he'd moved on assuming she hadn't cared.

A divorce.

He'd wanted a divorce.

"Oh-my-God!" Her breath escaped and Clayton took a step away from her.

"What?"

She could see the fear in his eyes. He was ready to run and collect his girls if he had to. She must have looked like a maniac.

"Adam wanted a divorce."

"Okay." He'd taken another step away from her.

"No, you don't understand." She moved to the kitchen table where the boxes of letters from Adam sat. She walked her fingers through the envelopes, which she'd filed in order. When she found the one she wanted, she pulled it out. "Look. He wants a divorce. He wants to move on."

Clayton took the letter and scanned over it. "Vivian, I don't understand."

Of course, he didn't. She was sounding like a lunatic.

She put her hands up as if to signal for herself to stop. "He wanted a divorce because he wanted to move on. He went about it a bit too quick, if you ask me."

"Men will do that—usually."

She took the letter back and looked down at it. "You don't understand. After I'd learned that he'd married two other women, we found out that my marriage and Penelope's marriages had never been filed."

"You weren't married?"

She shrugged. "By then common law, but no. We had never been married."

"So what's all this about?"

"He wouldn't have asked for a divorce if he'd known he wasn't married."

Clayton moved from in front of her, picked up his coffee mug, and sat down at the table. A positive sign, she thought. Maybe she wasn't so crazy now.

"So, your husband married you, but it wasn't filed."

"Right."

"He assumes you're not communicating with him," he points to the boxes of letters. "So he asks for a divorce."

"Yes."

"So he assumed he was married."

"Yes!" Okay, good, he'd been paying attention. "That means his mother had been screwing with us since day one. She wanted me to live here while he was away so that she could keep an eye on me."

"Why?"

"I don't know. She's a freak."

He actually chuckled at that then stifled it with a sip of his coffee. "And you think she's the one that broke into the house?"

"If not her, she's behind it."

"But she's in rehab?"

"I can't find proof of that. I don't know where she is."

"But she could be trying to get to you right now?" His voice was straining.

VIVIAN

"Don't take your girls away."

He bit down on his lip. "I won't. But I'm not going anywhere either."

"What does that mean?"

Clayton stood and moved directly in front of her. He didn't touch her, but his eyes locked into hers. "I'm going home. I have to gather a few things. And then I'm coming back here to stay with you. And when you move to the other house I'm coming with you."

Vivian stared at him for a long silent moment. "You're moving in with us?"

"Just for a little bit. I want to be here. When you're working, you'll have Penelope and Amelia around. Amelia would kill anyone who hurt any of you—or my girls."

She felt her lips tremble. "You'd do that for me? For us?"

Clayton lifted his hand to her cheek. "Remember, I'm bad with hints. I'm very interested in you. I'm not just looking for someone to make me forget Linda. I'll never forget Linda. You'll never forget Adam." He kissed her softly. "You should never forget Adam."

Chapter Nine

Clayton had left the girls with Vivian and headed back to his house to collect his school bag for tomorrow, as well as some clothes for the girls. And dare he forget the pink blanket for Stephanie and Boo-Boo Bunny for Charlotte.

There was no way he'd tell Vivian he was worried about Adam's mother, but he was. What kind of woman keeps a man and wife apart? What would she have done if Adam hadn't have died?

It was natural for him to second-guess everything now that Linda was gone. He'd met the young man she'd taken care of a few times. He'd just been a sad young man. Never in his wildest dreams did he think that the boy would become some murdering lunatic.

You never knew when someone would snap and he was going to be there just in case something happened with Adam's mother.

Clayton scrambled through the hallway picking out items for the girls to wear. He backtracked to the bathroom and collected brushes and toothbrushes.

In passing through the living room, he stopped cold in his tracks and looked at the picture of their family. Linda's smile seemed to catch him and he moved to it.

"Oh, what am I doing?" He reached out and touched the picture. "I miss you so much," he said as he traced the outline of her beautiful face. "When I'm with Vivian the hurt isn't quite as bad."

VIVIAN

There was an ache in his heart. He needed to say the words aloud so that he heard them. Maybe she'd heard them too.

As he stood there in his meek little home, staring down at his wife's face, Vivian crossed his mind and he felt a smile form on his lips.

It was okay to feel this out with her. It was time to move on. In his heart, he knew Linda understood.

Vivian was frantically unpacking bags from the girls' room. They each wanted Stephanie and Charlotte to have certain stuffed animals to sleep with. They wanted to sleep all together on the floor of their bedroom with certain blankets. And of course, she had begun to freak out. A man was coming to spend the night.

She'd only ever slept with Adam, both sexually and literally.

Could she have a man in her bed?

Did she snore? Did she drool? God, what other things might she do that she didn't know about.

Was she ready to have sex with the man? He hadn't offered sex, she reminded herself. He'd offered her protection and security. And he wouldn't do that kind of thing with his kids in the house, or hers. Her mind was getting away from her. She was in no position to be thinking about sex from a man—this man. He'd said they were friends. She needed to keep thinking of it in that way. But his kisses had said differently to her heart, which had been aching for years.

It still meant she needed to find the clean set of sheets she'd packed and put them on the bed. She was going to be prepared for anything.

When Clayton walked through the front door carrying Barbie backpacks and a duffle bag, he was nearly mauled by the four little girls grabbing at him.

"We staying?" Charlotte burst out in question.

"Yes. One big slumber party."

"Swumber party!" she joyously added as if she knew what that really meant.

"Are you going to marry my mom?" Emma had her hands fisted on her hips looking up at him after the other three girls had run toward the bedroom.

Vivian covered her mouth as she watched his face contort into one of shock.

"Well…um."

"Penelope is having Daddy's baby. Are you and my mom going to have a baby?"

"Oh! Well…we haven't talked about that." His cheeks had gone straight to red and his eyes were wide.

"I think Penelope is having a sister. If you marry Mommy then, I'll have four sisters. I think I'd like a brother."

Clayton looked at her with a look of horror before turning back to Emma. "A brother is nice. Maybe Penelope will have a brother instead."

Emma shook her head. "No. That's for you and Mommy." And with that she retreated with the others to her bedroom.

VIVIAN

The burst of laughter that escaped from Vivian couldn't be helped.

"I'm so sorry. I didn't know she was going to quiz you."

"That was intense."

"You teach third grade. I'm sure you get worse."

"Yes, well it never has anything to do with me having sex with their mothers."

The laughter that rolled from her came harder. "I'm so sorry." When it moved through her—cleansed her—she let out a breath. "I laugh more when I'm with you."

"You also cry and get upset."

"Hmmm, I was trying for the compliment."

Clayton moved to her. "Listen, lady." He tucked his hand up into her hair. "I have a lot on my plate. I have two little girls, a demanding job, and a whole bucket full of new feelings. That little girl is wanting a brother. What am I going to do about that?"

The humor in the moment was gone and fear pierced her in the chest.

"Clayton, stop."

He dropped his hand. "I'm sorry. I was just..."

"I know. You were just kidding. I just don't know how to handle it."

He raked his hands through his hair. "Can we set some terms here?"

"Terms?"

"Yes. I'm mourning my wife and my life. You know that. You're in a whole different kind of mess with your mourning," he said holding his finger up. "And just go with me. I'm not saying you're a mess. It's just different."

She gave him a nod and urged him to continue.

"I like you." He let out a solid breath. "I mean, I really like you."

She didn't laugh, but a smile forced its way onto her lips. "I like you too."

"Well, now we're making some positive moves." He wiped his hands on his thighs. "I can't tell her we'll get married and those girls will be her sisters. That wouldn't be fair."

"We haven't known each other long enough for that."

"Right. But you need to know that when I'm in a relationship, I'm very serious about it."

"Honorable."

He moved to her and gathered her hands in his. "What I'm saying is, I've never been with anyone but Linda. I'm no good at this. I've never played the field. Had a one-night stand. Nothing. When I'm with someone, I'm *with* someone."

She nodded trying to keep up with his babbling. It was what he did when he was nervous. It was what she did too. What a pair.

"Clayton, I've never been with anyone but Adam. And that's been a long time. Even when he wasn't here I never went looking or moved on. I guess that was his way." She shook her head as if to erase the thought. "That's not fair. Now that I know what was going on."

"I think we're on the same page. When either of us enters a relationship, we're serious about it."

VIVIAN

"Right."

"I want a relationship with you."

A smile found its way back to her lips. "I'm not an easy person to have a relationship with. I'm sure Amelia and Penelope can vouch for that."

He laughed easily. "I'm willing to see how it goes." He moved in closer. "What I'm saying is I want to try. I'm not asking for marriage or little brothers. I'm asking you if you'll be mine for now. Let's heal together. Let's move on together. Let's see what comes."

Oh, this man was a peach. What had she done in her life to have God deliver him to her door—literally?

"So I'm your girlfriend?"

"Dear Lord, if you'll have me."

Vivian released her hands and wrapped them around his neck and he in turn around her waist.

"I feel like I'm ready for this. The last time I was with Adam I got Ava. So it's been a real long time since I've been with a man in any kind of relationship."

"I'm true to my word. I won't mess around. If things don't work out it'll be something we decide."

"And if they do?"

His cheeks reddened again. "Well, wow. I guess we could talk about baby brothers."

Vivian pulled him into her arms tighter and kissed him on the cheek. "You're going to make it much easier for all of us to heal."

"I can't think of a better way to celebrate love that you once felt than by doing it all over again."

"I'll never be Linda," she said as if he needed to know.

"I'll never be Adam." He kissed her gently. "But they need to know him. They need to know the good and joy of him."

She nodded. That would take some work. She'd been mad for too long. "You're right. I'm going to work on that."

He kissed her again. "Okay, now that that's settled can I have a pillow and a blanket for the couch?"

There was more than a little disappointment that ran through her. "You don't want to share my bed?"

"Not yet. They need to get used to us first."

He was making it very easy for her to move on from her pain. She could easily tumble in love with this man just by the way by the way he thought.

"I'll get you a pillow and a blanket then. I hope you don't mind *My Little Pony*."

He chuckled. "I wouldn't have it any other way."

As she turned out of his arms to find the bedding, he reached for her. "Have a date with me."

"Okay, how?"

"Would we be able to talk Amelia and Penelope into watching all the girls?"

Now she chuckled. "That's a tall order for anyone."

"I know."

"I'm sure I could arrange it."

"I may not want to sleep in there tonight to make things appear appropriate, but don't be fooled, I'm a man and in that bed with you is exactly where I want to be."

VIVIAN

Her heart beat nearly jumped out of her chest and the rest of her insides went to goo. There'd be no way they'd say they wouldn't watch the girls, she'd make sure of that. Because for the first time in her life she was pretty sure a man wanted to make love to her. It wouldn't be first love sex, angry makeup sex, or expected sex. Just the thought of it had her giddy with anticipation.

Chapter Ten

When Vivian's alarm sounded at the unholy hour of five o'clock in the morning, she promptly turned and silenced it with a shove off the nightstand.

Perhaps the horrible act of getting up and getting to work by six-thirty wouldn't be so bad when she actually lived in the house in which she'd worked. But for the next few days, at least, this was her new routine.

Penelope had solidified three more enrollments. By nine o'clock, there would be seven children under the age of five in their care. When the thought began to terrify her, she remembered that two of those kids were hers and two of them were Clayton's. The day would be just fine.

Clayton, his image ran through her head and she sighed. Then she realized it wasn't just his image, he was standing in her doorway in his pajama pants, a cup of coffee in his hands.

"I thought you could use a kick start. Something told me you're not a morning person."

He walked in, slowly extending his arms out to hand her the mug.

"You're an angel," she sighed as she took the mug and lifted it to her lips. "I have never had coffee brought to me in bed."

There was a low growl that came from him which had her lifting her eyes to him. "I'll keep that in mind since I'll be here."

VIVIAN

He sat down on the edge of her bed and a deep need surfaced in her. The last time she'd seen Adam, he'd sat down in the dark on the bed just like this. They'd had enough sex for nearly a year in the twelve hours he'd been home, but when he'd sat there, in the dark just as Clayton was doing, he was there to tell her he needed to leave.

Tears stung her eyes and she was grateful for the dark. "I was thinking, I don't have to be to school until almost eight. Why don't I bring all the girls then?"

She sipped at the coffee again. Here he sat on her bed and he wasn't talking about leaving, he was talking about staying and helping.

"I couldn't do that to you."

"You're not doing anything. You'll be with all the girls all day. Go, get settled in. Let me get everyone up and ready."

There should have been an alarm that went off in her head. It was bad enough that she'd let him sleep in her house and she'd thought of all those things she could do with him in her house. But no siren went off. Instead, a calm took over and she leaned into him.

"Are you sure?"

He tucked a piece of her hair behind her ear and she shuddered to think of how she must look.

His hand lingered and he caressed her face. "I'm very sure. Remember, I'm not going anywhere. If this all works out I'd want this routine in my life."

Vivian took a breath and realized how freely the air filled her lungs. He gave her that release, that moment of freedom.

"Thank you."

"You have no idea what kind of pleasure I get when I soften you just a bit," he said as his hand brushed down her neck and over her shoulder. "Get your shower and get ready. Do you want anything to eat this early?"

"Just a piece of toast."

"That I can make. I was hoping you weren't too complicated."

That made her giggle as he stood and walked out of the room, leaving her with her fresh, hot cup of coffee.

During the drive to the old house on Main Street and Pine, Vivian had already decided that she didn't want this first shift ever again. They were all going to be there the full twelve hours every day until Penelope had her baby. But it was only proving one thing. Vivian was not a morning person.

Though, as she ate her toast with strawberry jelly on it, she smiled. If that man were to send her off every day like that, it wouldn't be a chore.

As she pulled up in front of the house, she looked at the clock. Was she late? Amelia, Sam, Penelope, and Brock were all parked on the street and the house was lit up. She hoped nothing else had happened on this day they were to open their doors.

She climbed from the car, gathered her bags, and ran up the front steps.

When she pulled open the door, she saw what they were all doing. The bannister of the staircase, which now had a gate at the bottom, was adorned with balloons. Welcome signs hung in each room. There were flowers by the door with names on them. They must be for the mothers, she thought.

She could hear commotion from the kitchen so she walked back to find the four of them hovering over a box of donuts.

"What are you guys doing?"

Amelia shoved in a half of a donut and looked right at her. "Waiting for you," she managed without any food falling out of her mouth.

"I didn't know you were going to do all this."

Penelope smiled sweetly. "Brock's mom is in town and she thought it would be a nice touch. So we did the balloons last night."

"What are the flowers?"

"For the moms."

That's what she'd thought. "What about the dads?" she asked, thinking of Clayton.

Amelia moved in closer to her and nudged her with her elbow. "We figured you were taking care of the dads."

That should have been one of those moments when she unleashed on her. It wasn't called for when she did things like that. But it obviously wasn't something to hide anymore.

"Not yet, but you'll be watching all four girls all night on Friday."

Amelia finished her bite and then wiped her mouth with the back of her hand. "Excuse me?"

"You heard me. I need you guys. I really need you," she stressed. "Clayton and I want a night *alone*."

Sam picked up a donut out of the box. "So there is something going on there?"

"We're working through it," she said in a very somber tone as she set her bags on a chair. "His wife was killed two years ago in a school shooting."

The very mention of it had Penelope in tears and Brock moved in quickly to console her.

"Damn," Sam said with a wince. "I'm sorry. I didn't…"

"It's okay. Things were headed that way from the minute he walked into this house. I got spooked by the wedding ring."

"I noticed he wore it," Penelope muttered against Brock's chest.

"It was in Seattle. This is his fresh start."

"Seattle?" Sam asked and Vivian nodded. "Kid killed another kid and shot a few more before he shot the teacher he had some romanticized thoughts over."

"That's her."

"Oh, damn. He seems pretty solid."

"I think his walls are pretty high. Just like mine." She reached for a donut. "But I think we could tear them down together."

Amelia let a smile form on her lips and it always softened her Vivian thought. "The girls all get along well?"

"They have already asked to be sisters. This was all on their own. Oh, and they've ordered a brother because they think Penelope is having a sister."

The very thought of the conversation Emma had with Clayton had her on the verge of hysterical laughter.

VIVIAN

"When I look at the man I think I could actually give them that."

She knew every eye was on her, but she just didn't care. Clayton North was her miracle and she was going to embrace him.

By seven o'clock all seven kids had been signed in and their first day had begun. She'd forgotten how much fun three-year-olds could be when there were a few of them. They colored, read stories, played on the new playground, had lunch, and then it was naptime. Perhaps it was the excitement of the day, but each of them fell asleep on their little cot within ten minutes. She was fairly sure that would never happen again.

Penelope sat in the rocking chair, her hands on her enlarged stomach. She'd volunteered to sit while they were all quiet for the next hour.

Vivian walked to the kitchen and sat down to rest.

"I'm going to be tired tonight, but I'm really having fun," she said even amazed to hear herself say it.

"Clayton looked cute getting all the girls out of the car."

"Doesn't really work though. We're going to need a different car," she thought, then looked up to Amelia grinning at her. "What?"

"We're going to have to get a different car. Did you marry the guy?"

"No."

"You're going to."

"Not for a long time."

"Whatever."

Now she was on her feet. She found that standing eye to eye with the woman made it seem more even. "I'm not like you two. I don't just go and marry a man."

"Don't knock it. You never know what you'll do."

"I won't do that."

Amelia just chuckled and remained positioned right where she was, leaned against the counter.

"I didn't say it was a bad thing."

No, Vivian was sure with Clayton it wouldn't be.

She let herself relax. "I'm scared."

"Why?"

Vivian moved back toward her chair and sat down. "He's hurt. I'm hurt. There's so much…junk."

Amelia grabbed her water bottle from the counter and sat down across from her.

"You're both human and it's okay to love again. I feel whole with Sam. And for the first time I'm thinking about things I never thought I would."

"Like what?"

Amelia smiled. "Family."

Vivian studied her. "You're pregnant?"

"Late."

"Pregnant."

"Not confirmed."

"Pregnant."

"Maybe."

"Happy?"

"Deliriously so."

VIVIAN

She could feel both excitement and jealousy run through her. She wasn't sure which one she was supposed to embrace. "What does he say?"

"To keep quiet until the wedding."

She decided that the happy feeling was going to win today. There was no room in her life for negative. "I think that's wonderful."

Amelia rested her hands on Vivian's. At that moment, Vivian was sure she was pregnant. Only something like that would soften Amelia enough to offer such a gesture.

"Something is bothering you. It isn't this new found love for Clayton. You're not even mad that I might be pregnant."

"You're pregnant."

"Unconfirmed."

"Hmmm," she hummed out. "Something crossed my mind yesterday when I was talking to Clayton." She looked at Amelia. "Adam asked for a divorce."

"Right. He wrote to you."

"Why? Why did he need a divorce? We weren't ever legally married."

She watched as Amelia's eyes opened wide. "He didn't know that."

Vivian shook her head. "I can't vouch for what he knew about his marriage to Penelope. For all we know that marriage was a sham so he could sleep with her."

"You can't ever tell her that."

"I never would." And that was a promise she'd forever keep. True or not. "Something happened to that marriage certificate."

"How could she do this to you? All these years?"

"When I went to Oklahoma City the other day I was looking for information on where she might be in rehab. I, of course, am no one, so I can't find her. And Frank won't return my calls."

"Maybe Darby has contacted them and he knows we think she's up to something."

"Maybe. I'll have to talk to him." She heard the stirring in the other room. "For now I'm going to focus on this business and getting moved in here. And Clayton living with us."

"He's living with you?"

"When I realized Adam had asked for a divorce I think I was on a bit of a rant. He wants to stay close until we know what's going on."

"And that's why he brought the girls."

"He slept on the couch."

"*Really?*"

"Really. He's that kind of gentleman."

"Maybe he'll never go back."

Vivian felt the smile that pushed at her cheeks. "Maybe not."

Chapter Eleven

Clayton packed up at school and drove by his house. He collected his mail, more clothes, and whatever was about to go bad in the refrigerator. He had nine more months on the lease. Perhaps he'd better assume Vivian was safe and move home, or move her in with him.

No. She needed to be at the old house. The girls should be enveloped in something that had a part of their father. The house would offer that. He'd run through these halls as a boy. They'd have a connection to it.

He'd promised Brock an hour of his help on the bedroom in the old house. Vivian would just be cleaning up and then they could head home.

He liked the thought of it. They. Home. The male hormones running through him wondered if she'd solidified a date for Amelia and Penelope to watch the girls. He had romantic plans for dinner and whatever she wanted to do after, but he was man enough to hope she really wanted to go home and do what men and women do.

It had been two years for him and at least as long for her. They both were two sexually pent up people.

When he pulled up in front of the old house, he climbed from his car and pulled out the bag of items he'd taken from his refrigerator. He'd store them in the kitchen until they headed to Vivian's.

The days were growing shorter and the daylight was already slipping away. Streetlights were already turning on and the house in front of him was illuminated. As he approached the house, he could hear small voices and laughs coming from inside. There was a lock on the front door, so he'd have to be buzzed into the house now that it had kids in it. He liked the idea. Even his elementary school had the same security. Everything was different now that kids took guns and weapons to school.

The very thought gave his heart a kick and the sickness of it jolted through his stomach. Before he hit the buzzer on the door, he took a moment to compose himself. He wasn't going to take any bad energy into the house with him.

Amelia hurried to the door, a paintbrush in her hand. "Oh, hey. I thought maybe you were Kelly's mom."

"Is she late?"

"No, Kelly is just ready to head home. She's had one very full day and has a lot to tell Mom about."

He smiled as he stepped through the door and let it close behind him. "That's good, right?"

Amelia nodded and crooked a finger for him to follow. They stood just out of sight near the room that had once been the dining room. Vivian sat on the floor with six little girls and one little boy playing what looked like hot potato. The kids laughed and the sweetest sound echoed in his ears—Vivian's laughter as she played with the kids.

"She was meant to do this," Amelia whispered. "She has a gift."

Didn't he know it? Just being with her the other night he'd calmed when she'd asked about Linda. He'd told her everything and he'd never done that before. Her hard exterior was from the hurt Adam had caused her. But he thought, in time, that would shatter and her hate for Adam would too. He'd be there to catch her when she had that fall, but when it was done, he was sure she'd always be as happy as she was on the floor with those kids.

Charlotte looked up from the game. He'd have expected her to run to him, but she didn't. Instead, she giggled and continued to play with Vivian and the other kids.

Amelia turned to Clayton. "Brock is upstairs working in the attic."

"I'll put this food away and head up."

Amelia started up the stairs as he headed back to the kitchen.

Penelope sat at the table with her feet propped up on another chair. She rubbed her stomach in small circles.

"How are you feeling?" He asked as he opened the refrigerator and placed the bag inside.

"I don't think he's going to hold on too much longer. A couple of weeks, max."

As he shut the door, he turned to her. "Who will give out first? You or the baby?"

She let out a small laugh. "I feel like a house. Look at my ankles."

He looked down at her feet and his first thought was *what ankles?* Of course, he replied, "That's normal. Let me get you an ice pack."

VIVIAN

Clayton opened a drawer and pulled out a storage bag. He went to the freezer and filled it with ice from the ice tray. Pulling the towel from the handle on the oven door, he wrapped it around the bag and then gently set it on Penelope's ankles.

"Linda's ankles used to swell like that. She carried the girls right out front. If you saw her from behind you'd never have known she was pregnant. But her ankles," he smiled, "they were always swollen."

"Linda was your wife?"

He keyed right into the word *was* as Penelope said it. It was something he'd never get used to.

"Yes."

She reached for him. "I'm sorry about your loss."

He gave her hand a pat. "Thank you. It's nice to finally be moving forward again."

She smiled up at him sweetly before she returned her hands to her stomach.

"Are you having contractions?"

She shook her head. "He's changing positions or something. We are not cohabitating well right now."

Clayton watched her as she adjusted with the baby's movement. Pregnancy was always a wonder to him. When Linda was pregnant, it had been hard for him to keep his hands off of her. He wanted to touch her all the time.

He'd seen Brock touch Penelope in the same way he'd touched Linda. The thought crossed his mind that Penelope and Brock would probably have another baby soon, just as he and Linda had.

It was then the pain of it all settled into his chest. They'd planned to have four children. Stephanie and Charlotte were only eighteen months apart. It was exactly how they wanted them spaced. The unfortunate realization was that Linda had to go back to work for them to afford another baby. How could they have ever known it would have been the one thing to destroy their lives?

"Are you okay?"

Penelope was looking up at him as he stood staring at her. "Sorry. I got lost in thought."

Clayton bent down and kissed her on the top of the head. "Yell if you need anything."

He headed out of the kitchen and up the stairs to help Brock.

Amelia was in the hallway painting the trim around the bedroom door. "You'd better help him before he hurts himself. He's determined to get that closet torn out. I don't know what he's doing."

"Building her a loft with a set of stairs."

Amelia looked as though she were processing the idea. "So turn the attic into a sitting room?"

"Right. Then other than the kitchen, they'll have a real living space up here."

She smiled wide. "He's genius."

"I heard that," Brock shouted from inside the room. "I could use some help."

Clayton moved into the room, which had been stripped of everything in it. "I'm glad you have a vision. I can't see anything of use in here."

VIVIAN

Brock chuckled from on a ladder in the hollowed out area that was once the closet. "Help me pull this down."

Clayton reached for the piece of wood, which Brock was working with and together they pulled off the board, which had framed the closet.

"This is going to take about a month to do on the schedule we have. She's going to have to stay in the other room until then."

"She could move in with me," Clayton said as he set the wood in the pile Brock had already started.

Amelia was quick to peek her head around the corner. "No. And I don't mean any disrespect with that," she added. "Penelope is having a baby in a few weeks. I'm getting married in a few weeks. We need her here and available. When everything settles down then…"

"I understand," Clayton nodded. "It'll be tight, but we'll all be okay here."

She narrowed her gaze at him. "You're worried something will happen?"

"Until you all know who was here that night and where Adam's mother is, she's not leaving my sight if she's not with you."

Brock climbed down off the ladder. "Sam's been looking for her." He rubbed his hand across the back of his neck. "I don't know if I'm supposed to mention what he does in his office."

Amelia pointed the paintbrush in his direction. "Spill it."

He nodded. "The Monroes are no longer living in Florida. Only, he doesn't know where they went."

"His dad is missing too?"

Brock nodded. "He learned that today."

Amelia looked back at Clayton. "Stay with her. We'll work hard to get this place fixed up. When I get back from my honeymoon then, she can move in with you."

He smiled. "I'll be happy wherever she is."

There was a sparkle that danced in Amelia's eyes even when her face was stone cold. "She deserves you. You make her happy."

"We're good for each other."

Amelia gave him a nod and went back to working on the trim.

Clayton picked up a broom and began to sweep.

They were good for each other. He'd never have thought that two broken souls could mend each other, but he believed it now.

Since the day he'd met her he'd felt at peace. He'd been searching for that for nearly two years. He wasn't fool enough to think that the pain would go away completely. He knew better. But he wanted the ache to go away. It had when he'd met Vivian.

"What in the hell?" Brock stepped down the ladder. "Holy cow, she was burying money in the walls too."

Both Amelia and Clayton moved toward him as he held out a handful of twenty-dollar bills.

"That's why there are holes in the walls," Amelia looked toward the closet.

VIVIAN

Brock nodded holding up a chewed bill. "I think the mice found a few of these."

Clayton watched Amelia bite down on her lip. "We need to get into that wall. Something tells me that someone knows that's in there. Because if they came for the box and then found a few of the books they know they don't have enough."

"You think they'll come back?" Clayton asked.

Amelia let out a long breath. "I do. We can't let her stay here." She stomped her foot and looked up at both of the men watching her. "We have to move the daycare."

Chapter Twelve

Vivian and Penelope had stayed on the main level until the last child was picked up. They couldn't imagine what the noise coming from the bedroom could be.

"Can you sit with the girls for a moment? I'll go see what's up," Vivian asked Penelope as her girls and Clayton's girls helped pick up the room.

"Sure."

Vivian started for the stairs just as the buzzer on the door rang. She looked back to see Sam standing on the porch.

She hurried back and opened the door for him.

"Did you have a harried day? You look frazzled," he said smiling at her.

It was then another loud thud came from the room above them.

"What in the hell are they doing up there?" he asked and then censored his question when he saw four sets of young eyes, and Penelope's, shoot a look his way. "I mean what the heck?"

"I was just headed upstairs to find out."

Vivian turned from him and they both hurried up the stairs.

Dust filled the air and she could see Amelia, Brock, and Clayton in the closet of the bedroom pulling at a piece of the wall.

"What are you three doing up here?" She stood with her hands on her hips, watching with Sam at her side.

Amelia stepped away from the wall and pulled a dust mask off her face.

"She hid money in the walls. There's at least a few grand here alone."

VIVIAN

Vivian was sure she couldn't blink as she stood there looking at her. "You're kidding."

Clayton walked toward them. His entire head was covered in dust and debris. "She's not. Look."

In his hands were small bundles of money, which had once been banded.

Amelia smiled. "Each one of these has a hundred dollars rolled up. It's almost as if the wall is insulated with it."

Sam stepped fully into the room. "Why were you tearing up the wall anyway?"

Brock stepped out of the closet and shook the dust from his hair. "Remodel." He smiled. "The steps to the attic aren't safe. I thought if she was going to live in this house she should have her own sitting area up there and it could be a loft from in here."

Sam's expression changed. "I didn't realize you were so handy."

"Can't say I knew either, but it seems to run in my blood." He smiled and headed back into the closet.

Amelia moved closer in toward them both. "You know what this means don't you?"

"I have to sleep with the girls longer," Vivian laughed as she spoke.

Amelia shook her head. Her face had gone somber. "Someone knows there's more money in this house. Having whatever they found in the box and in the few books they knocked over isn't going to hold them for long."

"You think they'll come back?"

Amelia nodded. "You can't stay here."

Vivian dropped her shoulders. "Right."

Amelia looked up at Sam. "We need to move the daycare," she said and her voice dropped. "It's not safe."

The air in the room had grown thick. They'd worked so hard for this and now they had to change everything all over again. It wasn't fair. This had gone on too long.

"She needs to be stopped. This is ridiculous. I can't keep uprooting my girls because their grandmother is a psycho."

Sam rested his hand on her shoulder. "All the more reason to do it. I searched all day for her. I can't find a single rehab facility that she's in. I also can't locate Frank."

Clayton stepped forward. "You'll stay with us. We have the room. The girls will be fine." He reached for her hand. "I want to do this. I don't want you to think about it too hard."

She gave his hand a squeeze. "What do we tell the other parents?"

They'd ordered pizza, which Vivian hated to do for the girls, especially since they'd just eaten out a few days earlier. But there was a need to make new plans.

"We only have three other kids, aside from your four." She looked at Vivian and Clayton. "Two families so far are displaced. I'm going to call Ann from the rec center at home and see about integrating our kids into their program for a few weeks."

"What are we going to tell those families?" Vivian raised her eyebrows at the concept of just moving their business.

"The house has been under renovation for months now. They know the work we've put into it. We'll just tell them we had an issue upstairs. We can be vague."

"I don't like this," Penelope said softly. "We've worked so hard."

Brock gave her shoulders a rub. "It's temporary until we know where Stella Monroe is and what she wants."

Vivian grit her teeth. "When I find that woman…"

VIVIAN

Clayton had his hands on her arms. "You'll do nothing. We let the authorities take care of it. For now, we make sure you're not in harm's way."

He was logical and she didn't know if that was a good trait or one she'd rather he lose.

Sam moved in toward the table to take another piece of pizza. "I'm going to follow up on a few leads I left untouched. Darby is being as cooperative as he can be. We'll figure it all out."

"Maybe she won't come back. It's been over a month," Penelope said softly. "We walked in on her—or them. Maybe they just gave up."

Vivian wished she had Penelope's optimism. But she didn't. Stella Monroe had been screwing with her for over a decade. Why would she stop now?

Clayton rubbed his hands down Vivian's arms. "Why don't we get the girls and head to my house? We'll stop and get some things for the night. Amelia call us when you know anything from the rec center."

"I will."

Vivian gave Clayton a nod and went to find the girls who were playing with the baby toys in the infant room.

Clayton ran his fingers through his hair and looked at the other couples around the table.

"I'll keep her safe. But let me know where I need her to be in the morning."

Amelia stood from her seat to meet his eye. "I don't know why that woman would do this. Except for the money buried in this house. Vivian deserves better."

"I plan to give her that."

Sam stepped in closer to Amelia. "I'm glad you happened along." He held out his hand to shake Clayton's.

"I believe in fate," he said shaking Sam's hand.

When he walked toward the infant room, he could hear Vivian and the girls laughing as they put away the toys they'd been playing with.

"Who's ready to go home?" he asked and all five of them turned their eyes to him.

"Aw uf us," Charlotte said firmly.

"All of us. Tonight we're going to stay at our house."

That put a smile on her face as she grabbed for Ava's hand to do a little dance.

Vivian gave him a gentle smile as she continued to help the girls tidy the room.

He waited for Vivian to say her goodbyes and together they took the four girls out to their cars and buckled them in.

"I was telling Amelia this morning that we needed a new car. A mini van or something," she said as she closed the door on her car.

Clayton laughed. "Be careful. You're making us sound like an old married couple."

He walked toward her and wrapped her in his arms.

She rested her head on his shoulder. "I'm beginning to think it doesn't sound so bad."

He slid a finger under her chin and raised it so she was looking up at him. "I'm not sure it's worth being decent anymore. My couch isn't so comfortable."

He felt her swallow and then she moistened her lips. "Clayton, I don't know. What if…"

"What if those girls thought what they already do?" He moved his hand to cup her face. "They asked for this. They want this. I want this."

"What is this?"

Clayton moved in as a cool breeze swirled on the air. He pressed a kiss to her lips and let it linger just long enough to convey what he wanted it to. "This is the beginning for both of us. For them. Are you willing to start over?"

Now she shook in his arms. "It's not over for me yet. I don't have peace with Adam."

"I think you will."

"But his mother…"

"Isn't Adam." He pressed another kiss to her lips. "Adam didn't get the chance to see where all of his paths lead. I don't know how you could hate him when you have Amelia and Penelope. Or Ava and Emma."

Her lips tightened and he could see the tears swell in her eyes. "You're one of those people who looks at everything with rose-tinted glasses aren't you?"

He shrugged. "I would say I was. Until Linda died. I can't find right in that. I can't find peace in it. But when I'm with you I don't ache. I don't hurt. When I'm with you, I'm at peace with me."

Vivian lifted her arms and wrapped them around his neck. "I think your bed *would* be more comfortable to sleep in."

He pressed his forehead to hers. "I can't tell you how much I'd hoped you'd say that."

Chapter Thirteen

Vivian looked in her mirror at the two girls sleeping in her back seat. For years, they'd been her life. Every moment was about them, but had she really taken the time to focus on that?

Emma would start kindergarten next year. Where had the time gone?

Ava stretched and turned her head in her seat. She looked the most like Adam, but often Vivian refused to acknowledge that. But her blonde hair and her blue eyes matched his. She had his nose and that same dimple in her cheek.

Her heart clenched just a little bit when she thought about him.

It seemed so long ago that they'd loved each other. He'd been everything to her for so long. But the moment Emma was born it seemed as though he'd been replaced in her heart—and then he was gone. First he was stationed elsewhere and then deployed. They'd never had a chance to be a family.

Clayton's car stopped at a red light in front of her and she eased to a stop behind him. In her headlights, she could see him raise his hand and wave at her. She waved back and smiled.

In just the past week, she and Clayton had formed a family. How could that have happened? She didn't really know him, but she felt as though she did. The girls were in love with his girls and she was too. Every part of what they had seemed right, even if it was new.

As they eased through the light, she thought about sleeping in his arms tonight. She was sure he wouldn't mind keeping anything more intimate for the night they'd have

VIVIAN

alone. It would give her some time to think about what was going on in her mind—in her heart.

She was sure she knew though. She'd had this feeling as a young woman, but now it was much more intense.

The very thought of him made her smile.

His voice made her giddy.

His touch sent tingles through her.

She had gone and fallen in love with this man that just over a week ago she'd nearly yelled at for rescuing her off the side of the road.

Following Clayton down the street toward his house she wondered if it was time to tell him of her revelation. The very thought of it had her bubbling with anticipation.

She watched as he pulled into the driveway, but there was another car parked in front of his.

Her heart began to race as she watched a woman open the car door and step out into the street lamp light.

Clayton opened his door and stepped out of his car as she pulled to the curb. He walked to the woman and pulled her into his arms.

Vivian's heart lodged in her throat and tears stung her eyes. A moment later he was turning toward her and waving for her to come to him.

She clenched her jaw. Something told her she wasn't ready to get out of the car yet.

As Clayton walked toward her car, and the woman began to help his girls from his car, she shifted to park and took a breath.

He pulled open her door. "Are you coming?"

"Who is that?" Vivian looked past him at the woman bent over in his car.

A smile formed wide on his face. "It's Dorothy. Linda's mom."

She didn't know what to do with that. This wasn't the time for her to be at this house with the intent to sleep in his arms. Suddenly, she felt as though she was going to be sick.

"Why is she here?"

He shrugged. "I don't know. I think she misses the girls."

"You didn't know she was coming?"

"No. This was a surprise," he said still smiling.

"I should go back to my house."

Clayton reached for her arm. "Oh, no." He crouched down so he was face to face with her. "I'm not cheating on her daughter. This woman lost everything that day too and now I've taken her girls from her. She misses them. That's all. She called the other day and missed them more so she came to see them. I want her to meet you."

"She's going to hate me."

"Vivian," he said capturing her attention and then her face in his hands. "It's time for us all to move on. She needs to meet the woman I love now."

For a moment, she was sure she'd forgotten to breathe. What had he said? No. No. She was supposed to tell him how she was feeling. But this wasn't the time.

She looked past him to see a woman who resembled Linda, only about thirty years older, standing behind him with Charlotte and Stephanie holding her hands.

Clayton rose to his feet. "Dorothy, this is Vivian."

She was in an awkward position now, she thought. Unbuckling her seatbelt, she managed to slide from the car without getting caught up in the strap.

"Hello," she said softly.

"Hello." Dorothy smiled. "I hope I didn't ruin any plans, but after I called the other day I began to miss my girls so much I thought my heart might break."

"Dorothy," Clayton's voice shook as he said her name.

VIVIAN

She shook her head. "No, don't go apologizing. I understand why you left Seattle. I don't blame you one bit. I'm allowed to miss you all too. We all have to heal and it's going to take longer than two years to do that, I'm afraid."

Clayton turned to Vivian. "Let me help you get the girls in the house."

"Oh, I should just head home. You two should catch up."

Dorothy smiled. "Clayton, I'll take these two inside."

He nodded, handing her the keys to the door before turning back to Vivian as they walked away.

She could feel the urge to cry and perhaps even yell—though it wasn't warranted.

He pulled her into his arms as if he knew what she was feeling.

"There is one thing that happened when I married Linda. I married into this family who believes in forgiveness, second chances, love at first sight, and giving everyone an opportunity to prove how good they can be."

"What are you talking about?" she murmured against his chest.

"Dorothy is the kind of woman who isn't going to judge us. C'mon, she already knows there's something going on. How could she not?"

"This doesn't feel right."

"It doesn't feel wrong either." He pulled back, but she stopped him.

"What did you say to me before you introduced us?"

Clayton's eyes widened. "Is this a test? I don't…"

"You said she should meet the woman…"

He smiled. "Right." He took her hands in his and laced their fingers together. "I said she should meet the woman I loved."

113

Vivian let the air whoosh out of her lungs. "I thought that's what you said."

"Does it bother you that I feel that way?"

She shook her head. Her stomach felt as though a million butterflies had just taken flight inside of her. "I was thinking the same thing as I was driving over here."

"You knew I was going to say I loved you?"

She laughed easily. "No. I realized that I'd fallen in love with you."

Clayton moved in and kissed her gently. "Dorothy is going to be okay with hearing that."

"What about you?"

He raised her hand to his chest and slipped it under his jacket, pressing it firmly over his shirt. "Can you feel that?"

She could. His heart rammed in his chest as hard as hers was.

"I know the timing is awkward, but I think there is a lot to explore with these feelings. I hope you'll tell me you love me again and again."

Clayton carried Emma into the house and Vivian carried Ava. "We'll lay them in the girls' room. My girls won't be too far behind them to sleep."

Once they were situated, he took her hand and walked with her to the living room where Dorothy was seated with his girls reading a book.

"We're just catching up with some *Max and Ruby,*" Dorothy said.

"Mommy's favorite," Stephanie added and Clayton felt Vivian's hand squeeze his.

"It was her favorite." He moved closer to them, still holding tight to Vivian. "Why don't the two of you go put on your pajamas, quietly, and then you can come see grandma some more."

They gave him a nod and ran off to their room.

"Dorothy, can I make you some tea?" he asked.

"That would be lovely. Perhaps Vivian would keep me company for a moment."

Clayton gave her a nod. He knew she was hesitant, but Dorothy would never, ever, say anything to hurt Vivian. In fact, he thought if he left them alone just long enough he'd come back to Vivian's smile. Dorothy had that kind of effect on people.

Vivian moved to the couch and Clayton walked to the kitchen. He figured it was a good that they hadn't been in the house for the past few days. The dishes were still clean. Dorothy would never say a word about how their house was kept, but he'd want her to be proud of him. It was important.

As he filled the teapot with water, he heard Dorothy laugh and then Vivian laugh. Yes, that was what he'd expected.

When he finally had three cups of tea made, and balanced in his hands, he walked back to the living room.

Both girls had climbed up on Dorothy and fallen asleep. Vivian jumped up and helped him with the mugs. She set two of them on the table and he set the last one down as well.

"Let me get them to bed," he said moving to pick up Charlotte.

"I'll get Stephanie," Vivian moved toward her.

Dorothy kissed them both on the head as they were carried to their room.

They had laid Vivian's girls on Stephanie's bed, so they laid his girls on Charlotte's.

"This is when I'm glad they both can sleep in normal sized beds." He laughed quietly.

"Twin beds are not normal."

"We're going to have to figure out what to do when you move in here."

She'd bitten her bottom lip, but she didn't say anything. They still needed to talk. He knew that was coming.

Clayton pulled the door behind him as he walked to the living room, leaving it open just a crack.

"I'll bet your girls all get along beautifully," Dorothy said from the couch as she sipped her tea.

Vivian picked up her mug and sat down in the chair. Clayton picked up his and sat next to Dorothy on the couch.

"They do," he said smiling. "They want to be sisters."

"Hmm," Dorothy smiled from behind her mug. "Wouldn't that be precious?"

"We haven't made any plans," Vivian was quick to add, her eyes darting from Dorothy to him.

"Oh, don't be nervous about me," Dorothy laughed. "I could tell there was something going on the moment you pulled up. I'm happy for Clayton. I really am."

He gave her a knowing grin before turning his attention back to Dorothy. "How long are you visiting?"

She shrugged. "I don't know. At least a few days," she said. "I'm missing my girl. I'm missing my granddaughters. I sometimes think I should have come with you."

"You would miss your water."

"I would." She grinned. "I love my rain."

"I should let you two catch up," Vivian said setting her mug on the table and standing. "I'll go pull up some floor in the girls' room."

Dorothy shook her head. "Oh, I'm no prude. Don't you sleep together?"

Clayton could feel his cheeks heat and he assumed they matched the red in Vivian's.

116

VIVIAN

"We haven't gotten to that stage in our relationship yet," he said. "I've been staying with her because of her mother-in-law. She's a little unstable."

Dorothy nodded. "She told me about that."

He figured they'd hit it off in those five minutes of him in the kitchen. They'd discussed *everything*.

"Well, I'll take this couch. It always was comfortable," she laughed. "Tonight would be a good night for the two of you to figure out who steals the sheets."

Vivian's eyes were wide and her mouth hung open. Clayton couldn't say he'd ever seen her at a loss for words.

"Let me get her settled then and I'll bring out bedding for you."

He stood and reached for Vivian. She gazed up at him. "Can I have just a moment?"

"Yes." He kissed her cheek and headed to his bedroom.

"My mother-in-law seems to have tried to ruin my life. We were never close. She never really cared for me much. I just wanted to say that you are delightful," he heard her say from the hallway. "I'm so sorry for your loss. I can't imagine what you're going through. And to be gracious to me when I'm here with Clayton...well..."

He could see Dorothy stand from her seat. "I know a good person when I see one. You're a good person. I don't want Clayton alone forever. Linda wouldn't have wanted it either. I can tell, you make him happy."

"I haven't known him long."

"How long do you really need to know someone to love them?"

He thought his heart might explode. Quickly he stepped into his bedroom and waited for Vivian.

She was wiping her eyes as she walked toward him. "She's lovely," Vivian said.

"I know."

"This still seems awkward. Me sleeping here with you."

"You're only sleeping. And if you want me to I can…"

"You can sleep in here with me." She moved to him and wrapped her arms around his neck. "I watched Amelia and Sam fall in love and thought they were moving too fast. But it worked. I watched Penelope and Brock fall in love in a few weeks and thought this doesn't really happen."

"And now?"

She rested her head against his chest. "I've been so lonely for so long I'm afraid I'm doing the same thing, but now I wonder if it's real."

Clayton pushed back from her to look at her. "Honey, it's real." He moved his hand to her cheek. "Why wouldn't it be?"

"I'm not used to things feeling right. This feels right."

He chuckled softly. "What could possibly be wrong with that?"

Vivian shrugged. "Amelia and Penelope ran off and married Adam on a whim. They just took a chance. And then they each took another. I've never taken a chance in my life."

He pulled her in again. "Maybe you should."

"Maybe I should."

Chapter Fourteen

Clayton settled Vivian into his room and closed the door as he walked back to the living room with sheets and a pillow in hand.

"I hope I didn't put you out," Dorothy said as she stood from the couch.

"I promise, you'll never put me out. I'll always open my door to you—anytime." He set the sheets on the couch. "My tea is cold. Can I offer you another cup?"

"Oh, I'll be up using the bathroom all night, but you know, I'd really appreciate another cup. I'll come in with you."

She followed him to the kitchen and made herself at home at the kitchen table.

"She's lovely, Clayton."

He smiled to himself as he filled the teapot. "She is, isn't she?"

"Very strong willed I think."

Now he chuckled. "Very."

"You're going to marry her, aren't you?"

He wasn't sure what he was supposed to do with that question. Her voice was solid, but how did he tell this woman that yes, in fact, he'd thought about it a lot.

He set the teapot on the stove and turned to face her.

"I don't know what to do with the thoughts I have on that. Linda has been gone for two years. Her husband has only been gone for four months."

Dorothy nodded. "She told me her husband had married three women."

"You two got a lot of talking in earlier."

"I don't beat around the bush. I never have."

He smiled. No, Dorothy had always been straight forward.

"Yes. He married two other women. They both have already become engaged to other men."

She rubbed her hands together. "So quickly?"

The teapot behind him whistled and he removed it from the heat. Pouring himself a mug full and filling Dorothy's, he said, "Lots of circumstances."

"Tell me."

He set the pot back on the stove, grabbed tea bags, and sat down with her at the table.

"Vivian hadn't really seen him since Ava was born."

"She has to be two years old."

"She is." He dipped his tea bag into the water. "And in fairness, because of this stuff going on with her mother-in-law, he'd asked for a divorce to marry Amelia."

"She didn't give him one?"

He shook his head. "She didn't know he'd asked." He went on to explain about the box of letters they'd found in the attic of the old house. "He assumed she'd given up on him."

"That's horrible."

"Anyway, he married Amelia and two years later she found out about Vivian and she asked for a divorce."

"Good for her."

"So really, Amelia had moved on a long time ago."

"And the other?"

"Penelope. She married Adam in April and then he was deployed. She's due to have a baby in December."

Dorothy reached her hand to Clayton's. "That's very sad."

"It is, but Adam had only met her. They dated two weeks before they ran off and married."

"He was a stranger to her."

"He was. Then when he was dying he asked the soldier who was holding him to find her. Well, he did and they've fallen in love."

Dorothy placed her hand on her chest. "That is very sweet."

"He had a lot of respect for Adam and he wants the baby to know all about him. They've already decided the baby will carry on his name in some way."

"I'm moved."

He could see she was. Her eyes were misting.

Clayton sipped his tea to test the strength before pulling the bag out and setting it on a napkin.

"When you consider that Adam and Vivian haven't seen each other since Ava was born, and only then when they conceived her..." He lifted his mug to his lips and swallowed his tea hard enough he coughed. "Well, he's been gone from her for a long time."

Dorothy reached her hand out to him and placed it on his arm. "Are you afraid you're being unfaithful to Linda or to Adam?"

Clayton clenched his jaw. "Yes. How could I not feel that way, especially with you here?"

She nodded as if she understood he'd feel that way. "I miss her more than anything. There are days I can't breathe."

He knew that feeling well enough.

"Clayton, you have a second chance. Do you know how happy I am for you? If it could be Linda all over again, I'd wish for Linda. But we both have to keep living and keep her memory alive for those girls. And those girls will be better off if you're happy and can keep her memory a happy one."

VIVIAN

Clayton wasn't such a man he wouldn't cry. He could feel the tears sting and catch in his throat. "I love her Dorothy. I love Vivian."

"I know you do. And what the hell does it matter if you've only known her a short while? You could know her forever and still never be sure." She smiled and it calmed him.

"I want to take her away from here for a few nights. She's never left this town in years. I want to feel it out—see what happens."

Dorothy stood from her seat and rested her hands on both sides of his head as she lowered a kiss to his forehead. "I'll stay as long as you'd like me to. I'll be here for the girls. I have a feeling all four of them are going to be equally as important to me."

Clayton was going to pay for yet another late night. It was nearly midnight when he and Dorothy had stopped talking. Third graders might be the death of him in the morning.

He pushed open his bedroom door and the moonlight from the window fell over his bed. Vivian lay on his pillow breathing softly.

His heart beat hard in his chest. She was a lovely sight.

Her dark hair fanned out over the pillow. Her bare shoulder shimmered in the moonlight. How was it he'd fallen into this job and into her life?

Things couldn't be more crazy and messed up for them than they already were. But he never wanted to walk into that room again without knowing she'd be there.

Clayton toed off his shoes and tossed his socks into the laundry basket. He unbuttoned his shirt as he watched her sleep. He tossed his shirt into the laundry as well and then slid down his pants. He looked around and wondered if he had another pair of pajama pants. He'd packed them for her house, but usually he slept in his boxers. Well, this was going to have to be one of those *normal* nights.

He walked to the bed, slid back the sheets, and climbed in next to her. She moaned and opened her eyes.

"I didn't know what side you slept on," she said with a sleepy haze in her voice.

"Whatever side you're not on."

"Hmmm," she moaned and rolled so that her back was to him.

He wanted to touch her. There was so much about an intimate relationship that he missed.

"Clayton, hold me," she whispered in the dark.

He moved in behind her and draped his arm over her as he pressed a kiss to her ear.

"I love you," she said softly as she drifted back to sleep.

Clayton lay there for a long time thinking about the conversations he'd had with Dorothy. How had he been so lucky to fall into that family? He'd wished Vivian had similar luck. Then again, if either of them had any luck at all, they wouldn't be where they were.

Vivian woke to the smell of coffee and she stirred. When her senses came to her fully, she sat upright in the bed and looked around. For a moment, she'd forgotten where she was. The room was sans of décor. A chair in the corner held Clayton's pile of clean clothes and a basket near the door held his dirty ones. There was a TV on a small stand against the wall, but that was nearly the extent of it.

She smiled when she thought of the girls' room with the pink walls and Barbie decorations on the walls. He'd done everything to make them comfortable in their home.

Panic rushed through her when she thought of the time. It must be nearly seven o'clock. She hadn't even checked in with Amelia or Penelope. There were obligations to the families that had hired them. Even if they moved their daycare, they had obligations.

And what about her girls? They needed to get up. And what would they think when she rolled out of Clayton's bed?

She pulled herself from the sheets and nearly fell on the floor when they tangled around her legs as she tried to stand.

Just then the door opened and Clayton walked through with a cup of coffee.

"You wake up rough, don't you?"

"The girls. Where are the girls? I have to get going."

He shushed her and anger began to zip through her, but he reached out a hand to touch her before she could let that anger fly.

"The girls are with Grandma Dorothy watching TV until I leave for work. Amelia called and the other two families have transferred to the rec center until you can open again." He handed her a cup of coffee. "Sam would like to see you in his office at ten."

She stood there with the cup of coffee clenched in her hands. "Are you always chipper in the morning?"

"No." He moved in closer to her. "However, my girls will tell you different. I never want them to see me wake up dreading the day. You never know how a day will end."

Her stomach clenched when he said those words. "I'm so sorry."

Clayton reached for her cheek and rubbed his thumb across it. "Don't ever be sorry. We are both here for the same reason. I don't suppose there will ever be a day when we don't stumble over each other's feelings."

"I don't think I loved Adam like you loved Linda. I don't suppose I'll ever miss him the same."

"Your mourning came before his death." He leaned in and brushed a kiss on her lips. "And I think in time you will realize just how much you loved him. And I'll be here to help you through that. Just as you've been here for me."

Vivian bit down on her bottom lip. "I don't think I've done anything to help you."

He smiled. "You have no idea."

He kissed her again. "I have to go. Grandma Dorothy has offered to keep the girls today if you're okay with that. She knows you have things to do."

"I don't know."

"You discuss it with her. She's a beautiful woman, Vivian. The girls will do great with her." He picked up his jacket from the chair in the corner. "She's keeping my girls today. Actually for a while. I think she wants to stay as long as she can."

"That's nice."

He moved to her again. "She's also going to keep my girls so I can take you away for a few nights."

Her breath caught in her lungs. "Just us alone?"

He brushed his fingers into her hair. "Alone." He moved in closer. "I miss the perks of a real relationship."

Vivian swallowed hard. "It's been a very long time."

"For me too." He pulled her close, minding the mug in her hand. "I'll never push you. But I'd give anything to be *with* you."

This time he gave her a harder kiss on the lips, though since she was very conscious of morning breath and she didn't deepen the kiss.

"I'll see you after school. I love you."

Her heart fluttered in her chest. "I love you too."

Chapter Fifteen

Vivian strolled into Sam's office at ten o'clock. The weight of the world seemed to be lifted from her shoulders for a while and it felt good.

The girls had begged to stay with Grandma Dorothy and she'd assured her that she'd take very good care of them. Though a little hesitant, Vivian finally had given into Dorothy's charm—and the girls' begging.

Brock sat at the reception desk taking a phone call. He gave her a wave and pointed to Sam's office.

Vivian smiled and headed back to the room where she could hear Sam and Amelia talking.

When she walked through the door both heads turned toward her.

"Good morning," she chirped. "I was thinking, where should we have Thanksgiving? It's a week away and we haven't planned anything."

Vivian walked toward the couch in Sam's office and sat down. "I know we can't run business out of the old house, but it should be big enough for everyone." She thought for a moment. "I wonder if Brock's family will be here. She's too close to having the baby to travel."

When she looked up, Amelia's eyes were wide on her.

Vivian couldn't help but smile at her. "How are you feeling?"

"I'm fine."

"No morning sickness?"

Amelia exchanged looks with Sam, who tucked in his grin before she hardened a look on Vivian. "Yes. Let's just keep that quiet, okay?"

"Right." The mood changed again in the room and she felt the need to stand up and move toward them. "Something's wrong. Is Penelope okay? Are you okay? Your baby…"

"Is fine."

"Confirmed?"

Amelia nodded. "Confirmed."

But the mood didn't rise in the room. "Something is up."

Sam reached for her arm. "Why don't we sit down?"

Vivian jerked her arm back. "Why don't you tell me what the hell is going on?"

"Where are the girls?"

"With Linda's mom." When both sets of eyes questioned her she continued, "Clayton's late wife's mother. It's a really long story. Tell me what's going on."

Again Sam and Amelia exchanged looks.

Sam took a deep breath and retracted his hand from her arm. "Frank called very early this morning. According to Frank, Darby was right. Stella was in rehab."

Vivian shook her head. "Well, at least we know she wasn't in the house. I'm glad she's getting help. Really I am. I mean…"

"There's more."

Vivian nodded and bit down on her lip to keep quiet.

"Frank called to let us know that she passed away while there."

Vivian's hand came directly to her mouth to cover the gasp that had escaped. "She's dead?"

Sam nodded.

She wondered how so many strange emotions could flood her at one time. Adam's mother was dead. But so was the grandmother of her children. But, if she were really dead then there was nothing to fear anymore. Things could go back to normal. And yet she was sad too. She didn't like Stella Monroe, but she'd been a big part of her life.

Vivian took a moment to gather her thoughts. "So we can move back into the house? If she's dead then…"

Sam held up his hand. "Frank says they're investigating the death as a possible homicide."

Vivian backed to the couch and sat down. "Why would…"

"He doesn't know. Darby told him about the break in and he assumes she was involved. Maybe they were covering their tracks. And maybe she just died. We don't know yet."

Vivian could only nod. Everything she was hearing was spinning in her head. She rested her head in her hands and just sat there.

"I'll get you some water," Amelia said and turned toward the small refrigerator in the corner.

"I don't want water." Vivian stood with anger boiling through her. "I want answers."

"We don't have any," Amelia shot back.

"I don't know what to do with this. First Adam and now Stella?" And then it hit her. Just as Clayton said it would. Adam was gone and she was finally feeling it.

Sam moved to her. "Sit down."

"Adam. He never knew I loved him."

"He knew."

She shook her head. "No. She kept him from me. She…"

"Shh." He looked toward Amelia. "Get the water."

He pulled her to him and she rested her head on his chest. "He wanted a baby, he did. Emma was his pride. Why didn't he tell anyone about her?"

"I don't know," Sam said rocking her against him.

"Brock held him. He held him in his arms as he died," she cried. "I never got to say goodbye to him."

VIVIAN

"You can. We can go out there."

She nodded as Amelia handed her the bottle of water.

"Sip. You need to calm down a moment."

Vivian sat up and took a sip of the water. "He left after seeing Ava," she sobbed. "He took one look at her and said, *she's not mine.*"

Sam wrapped his hands around hers, which held the bottle. "She is his, right?"

Vivian knew she should lash out at the accusation, but he was just being Sam.

"Of course she's his. I've never been with anyone else. Ever." She took another sip of the water. "I always wanted to tell him he was wrong. I wanted to tell him that we needed him and we wanted him."

"Did you write to him?"

She nodded. "But not to the address where his letters came from. He didn't know how I felt."

The tears fell freely and Sam pulled her to him. "I don't know what to say to make it better," he admitted. "I just know you have a man now who does love you and you can heal together."

She did. Yes, Clayton would help her heal. She could tell him all of this and she could be real about how she felt for Adam. Suddenly, she didn't hate him anymore and that was harder. When she'd hated him, she could forget him.

"Why don't I have Amelia take you back to Clayton's and you rest." It wasn't a question, but an order delivered in the calm manner Sam doled out. "Let's have dinner at the old house tonight and we'll plan Thanksgiving."

Sam kissed her on the top of the head and she sat a moment longer, just letting her heart ache.

Amelia drove her back to Clayton's house where the girls all played in the back yard and Dorothy kept a watchful eye on them.

"I want to go out and sit with them," Vivian said as she walked into the house and looked out back. "I feel the need to just be with them. All of them."

"Why don't you talk to Clayton about going out this weekend. I'll take the girls."

She smiled at the woman who should be her enemy. Amelia Monroe had a hard exterior that matched her own. How they ever broke through that she'd never know.

"I'd appreciate that. Dorothy is going to stay here for a while and she can take Clayton's girls."

"I still stand by the thought that if you get laid you might snap out of your funk."

She opened her eyes wide to stare at Amelia who was smiling at her. Amelia had said those words to her when it had become common knowledge that she was seeing Sam. Now it was laughable. And perhaps she was right.

"I have a class to teach. I'll take your car to the house tonight when we have dinner."

"I appreciate it. Tell Sam thank you—for everything."

"I will."

Vivian saw Amelia out. She then went to the kitchen for a glass of water before joining Dorothy on the back porch.

"They play really well together," Dorothy mused.

"They do. They want to be sisters and have entered an order for a brother."

Dorothy nodded slowly as Vivian sat down next to her. "I think they'd take good care of him."

Vivian laughed. "Children are innocent. They have no idea what is involved with building a relationship and having children. To them it all happens."

VIVIAN

"These four are special. They do get to have a say."

She looked at Dorothy. "It doesn't bother you that I'm here? You should hate me."

"I don't hate anyone, my dear. And it bothers me that Linda isn't around to see how big the girls have gotten. But I know she's watching over them and Clayton."

"I have a feeling I would have liked her very much."

Dorothy smiled. "I think you would have too. You remind me of her quite a bit."

That took her by surprise. She was sure she didn't hide it well when Dorothy chuckled.

"Your daycare center, for example. Even when Linda was a little girl she wanted to run a daycare. She babysat everyone's stuffed animals and when she was older she pet sat."

Vivian laughed now. "I did that."

"You're good with the girls. And they love you—all of them."

"I love all of them too."

"I think you and Clayton will be very happy together. I can't be sad over that."

Vivian reached out and placed her hand over Dorothy's. "You have no idea how much that means to me."

Dorothy patted her hand. "I'd love to be a part of it all. Linda was my only daughter. I could do with having another."

This time it wasn't just about smiles and a touch. Vivian stood and moved to Dorothy. She bent to hug the woman. Which angel was it that was watching over her, she wondered.

When the girls saw her hugging Grandma Dorothy they all ran over and joined in.

Vivian's heart, despite the sadness that still squeezed at it, was full of joy.

Chapter Sixteen

Vivian laughed at the girls singing *Silly Songs with Larry*, in the toddler room at the old house. Who thought an animated cucumber could ever be so funny, but the girls were enthralled.

Clayton had taken Dorothy back to the kitchen to meet everyone else.

Vivian walked slowly toward the back of the house where everyone gathered. There seemed to be a peace within the house now that she knew Stella was gone.

Her heart was still heavy and today, of all days, she actually missed Adam. She didn't care for Clayton any less, but she missed what she'd once had with Adam—when they had anything.

Penelope was seated in a chair with her hands on both sides of her stomach. "I swear I don't think I can get any larger."

Amelia laughed. "You're still four weeks away."

"Don't curse me," Penelope bit out. "I'm keeping my legs tightly closed for the next week. After that, I'm game to get this kid out of me."

Brock moved in behind her and rubbed her shoulders. "Just take it easy. We're all here to wait on you hand and foot. Don't move a muscle."

"I can't move a muscle."

Vivian let out a little laugh and looked toward Amelia who was watching Penelope. She could see her soaking in the moment. After all, in less than a year Amelia would look just as uncomfortable.

Vivian wondered when they'd announce the baby. But she was sure they'd wait until Penelope had given birth, if not after the wedding as they'd planned.

Brock looked up at Vivian. "Sam told us about Stella. I don't know what to say."

Vivian nodded. "It's been a bit surreal. But I feel peace here tonight. Do you feel it?"

Amelia raised her eyebrow. "Are you kidding?"

"Seriously. It just feels like we can go on again. We can finish the attic and the bedroom and get our business back. I loved being with those kids. I don't want to lose that."

Clayton smiled. "We'll get to work on it this weekend. But let's get the kids set up to eat. I'm starving and then we can plan Thanksgiving."

By the end of the night, they had decided on what everyone would bring to dinner. It was decided to have the meal in the house since the rooms could have tables set up in them. Brock's family would be heading out for the day and Amelia's father also had said he'd be making the trip.

Dorothy had promised to make the pumpkin pies and Clayton vouched for them as, "You'll never have a better pie. I swear."

That alone had clinched the deal.

The girls were easy to put to bed after playing all night long. Vivian shook her head as Clayton pulled the door on the bedroom. "They are going to need a better schedule."

"My girls are loving this," Clayton said. "I think I might have been too scheduled for too long."

Vivian chuckled. "One of the things I have learned from Amelia and Penelope is to enjoy the unexpected once in awhile."

"Finding your wild side are you?"

VIVIAN

She laughed and he loved it when she did. It brought a whole new side to her.

"I don't have a wild side. I have a perfectly planned side. A practical side."

"Me too." He walked toward the couch and pulled her down on his lap.

The sound of water from the shower could still be heard. He figured they had a few minutes before they needed to be appropriate around Dorothy.

He pressed a gentle kiss to her lips, which she warmly accepted. "I was thinking that our perfect plan might be to fix up the old house and all of us move in there. There is more room upstairs in that house than there is here."

She snuggled her head into the crook of his neck. "We'd have to remodel the kitchen."

"Most certainly," he said on a laugh.

Vivian sat up and looked at him. "What about this house?"

"I think Dorothy would like to stay for a while. I'm thinking of letting her stay here."

She lowered her head again. "I love her. You're a very lucky man."

Didn't he know it?

"I was also thinking, I have next week off of school for Thanksgiving. What do you say we make our evening out a couple full days?"

"I think I'd really like that if Amelia is up for it."

"Let's spend all of Tuesday together and most of Wednesday. Then the rest of the weekend can be for family."

"I really like how you think in that perfectly planned out mind of yours."

He pulled her closer to him. "Maybe we can find something to do that is unexpected and unplanned."

"I can't wait."

~*~

Once they'd had the conversation about how routine they both were, Clayton realized that was exactly who he and Vivian were. And that probably had a lot to do with the girls.

Kids needed routine and structure. There was a wake time, eat time, bed time. And as parents, they fell into that routine just as easily.

Their new routine, this week, had included working at the old house after work. He, Brock, and Sam had managed to get the closet wall torn out. The payoff was great. The house itself had netted over ten thousand dollars, which had been tucked in the walls. He wondered in time what else they would find.

They had collectively decided that they would wait until after the beginning of the year to reopen. That would give them time to finish the house—including the kitchen—and the upstairs. It would also ensure Penelope had her baby and give Amelia and Sam time for their wedding.

Clayton gave the house a little more thought. Perhaps he'd bring Vivian back there on their night together. He didn't want it to seem planned, but a few plans wouldn't hurt anything.

He could fill the finished room with flowers. Maybe he'd have champagne chilling in a bucket.

After all, even though they'd been sleeping in each other's arms each night, they still hadn't had much intimacy. It was hard to justify making love to a woman when your kids, her kids, and your mother-in-law were all in the other room.

The thought made him chuckle and Sam turned toward him.

VIVIAN

"Lost in your own thoughts?"

Clayton nodded. "I suppose I am."

Sam looked around the room. "I'll bet you guys could move back in here in another month. Maybe we can get it done in time for Santa to visit here."

Just the thought of it made Clayton light with excitement. Oh, he loved when Santa would visit him as a child. How glorious would it be for him to visit the girls—together.

"I'd love for that to happen."

"Then stop daydreaming and let's get busy."

Clayton laughed. Yes, he surely did believe in fate. Not only had moving to Parson's Gulch, Oklahoma given him a fresh start, it gave him much more. He had a woman he loved and two little girls that seemed to round out his little family just perfectly. Amelia and Penelope were more like sisters to him, and he'd even say that he'd become close enough to Brock and Sam he'd call them brothers. Who'd have thought he'd actually have found happiness when he moved to the small town?

He hadn't come for this bliss he'd found. He just wanted to be numb for a while and forget. But he wasn't numb—not at all.

Chapter Seventeen

Dorothy was in overdrive, Vivian thought. By Tuesday, she had baked four pies and was preparing for something else. The kitchen was abuzz when the doorbell rang and Vivian checked on the girls before answering it.

Sam stood on the doorstep with his sunglasses on and his hands clasped in front of him.

"Hey, what are you doing here?" Vivian asked. "Come in."

He didn't step in. "I need to talk to you—alone."

Vivian looked behind her and saw Dorothy peeking out from the kitchen and the girls on the floor coloring right behind her. She gave him a nod and stepped out onto the porch.

"Is Amelia okay?" She reached out and touched his arm. "Is the baby…"

He shook his head. "Everyone is fine. Where is Clayton?"

"Dorothy needed a few more items for dinner for the girls and for Thanksgiving. He's at the store."

He let out a breath and took off his sunglasses. His eyes were dark and his body looked heavy with dread. "I got notice today that Frank Monroe was found dead in his home."

Vivian sucked in a breath that stuck in her lungs. Tears filled her eyes instantly. "No. Why? What happened?"

He took both of her arms and held her. It was then she realized she was shaking. "Darby said it was an apparent suicide. I followed up with the local police department and they said that is the current ruling, but they are investigating it, especially after Stella's death."

Vivian lifted her eyes to meet his. "Someone killed her didn't they?"

He nodded. "They think so."

She felt her knees go week and she decided to sit down on the front step. Sam joined her.

"I don't want you alone."

She let out a grunt. "I'm never alone. I never was alone. Even when Stella and Frank were here I was never alone."

Sam ran his hand over his face. "I wonder if that too was by design."

She turned to look at him. "Are you kidding?"

Sam clasped his hands together and rested them on his knees. "The list of antidepressants and medications that Stella was on is extensive. Add alcohol and it's a sure sign she was running from something. I just can't help but wonder if they kept her medicated all these years for some reason."

How was it that suddenly Vivian was beginning to feel sorry for her? "Do you think someone was after her?"

He shrugged. "She did have a lot of issues with a lot of people in this town. Even Darby said he'd had a run in or two with her."

"Yes, but she was just a bitch. I don't think she was someone who could physically harm someone."

"Maybe she got involved in something. I mean, the woman had an affair and a baby from that affair while she was married. She seems to be good at being at the wrong place at the wrong time."

Vivian could hardly wrap her head around it all. "I can't believe they're both gone."

Sam reached behind his back and pulled his holster and gun from the band of his pants. "Here."

"Sam!" She looked around to see that no one was there. "Put that away."

VIVIAN

"I want it on you at all times."

"I could get in trouble with that."

"You could save your life if it comes to it. I have three more and I'll make sure all of you have them if I have to."

"I don't like this."

He motioned again for her to take it. "Do you know how to use it?"

She gave him another steely look. "I was married to a solider. There isn't much I can't do with a gun."

He smiled. "Okay then. Just keep it on you—in case."

"I don't want this with the girls around."

"Well, tomorrow you won't be with the girls. Use it to protect Clayton."

Her hands shook as she took the gun and set it on her lap. "With all due respect, I don't think he's going to look at me having a gun as a good thing."

"I know his wife was killed with one. But, damnit, Vivian, I don't want anything to happen to you or him—and especially those four girls. Until I know more, take it."

She nodded and slid the holster into the back of her pants just as Sam had. "Thank you for taking care of me."

"All of you are my family. No one—no one—gets hurt."

Vivian moved to kiss him on the cheek. "I love you. I can't imagine my life without all of you in it."

He rested his hand on hers. "You're never going to have to. Now I have to get back to work. Believe it or not, you're the next of kin. Stella's and Frank's ashes will be sent to you when the investigation is over. But I butted my way into the communication loop as your lawyer."

"I hope Adam covered that bill," she joked.

He smiled. "Paid in full."

Vivian closed her eyes tightly and took a moment to collect her thoughts. What a time for everyone to decide she was actually Adam's wife.

~*~

Vivian kept the gun that Sam had given her secured. The last thing she wanted was for the girls to find it. And she wasn't really sure what Clayton would think either.

As they packed for their night away, she slipped it into her suitcase and then locked the bag before putting it in Clayton's car.

She had dropped the girls off at Amelia's earlier that morning and now Clayton gave the girls instructions to help their grandmother.

For the first time they would be alone for two days and they'd be alone all night. Already her heart was pumping faster in her chest. Tonight Clayton wouldn't be just sleeping in the same bed. There would be no boundaries. They'd be alone and anything was game.

She rested her hand on her stomach. Funny, she couldn't remember being this nervous when she was seventeen.

Clayton looked at her. "Are you okay?"

She smiled. "Giddy. Nervous."

He took her hands in his. "I am too." He moved in closer to whisper in her ear. "I haven't had to buy condoms for years. I'm sure the clerk thought I might have a heart attack."

She laughed easily as he pulled her into his arms.

"I'm ready," she said softly.

"So am I."

They'd promised they wouldn't make plans. Everything would be spontaneous. Breakfast in Oklahoma City was more spontaneous than Vivian had expected.

VIVIAN

"Brock said there was some little dive near the courthouse," his voice was steady as he drove down the street. "He says it's old, run down, and has amazing biscuits and gravy."

Vivian laughed. "We drove this far for biscuits and gravy?"

"Hell yeah." He slowed the car. "There it is!"

He quickly pulled the car into a parking space on the street.

"I love that little things like this excite you."

Clayton unbuckled his seatbelt. "I'm glad. I like to take little adventures like this. Have you ever played the game where you flip a coin and heads you take a right and tails you take a left?"

She shook her head. "No."

"Then that's what we'll do when we leave. We have all night for playing games."

As they headed across the street, he took her hand. She loved this no-nonsense man who fed children knowledge, who doted on his daughters—and hers. He was hurt so deep inside, yet he could opt to love again. She'd be lucky if he'd have her for the rest of her life.

As he plowed through a plate of heart-stopping biscuits and gravy, she thought about his reaction to Frank's death. He'd been concerned, which she'd expected. But his compassion had touched her even further. The man didn't know Adam, or his parents, and yet he'd always had a kind word, which was more than she could say.

She hadn't told him about the gun, but he knew that Sam was worried about her safety. Clayton promised nothing would happen to her, but she didn't know what that really did to him inside if he knew about the gun.

His wife had been stalked by a fourteen-year-old boy, who eventually killed her. Was he as carefree about it when she'd friended him as he seemed to be hearing that maybe Frank and Stella Monroe had been murdered? Or was this his calm to keep her calm?

He'd had no problem leaving his girls with his mother-in-law. And equally, she felt as safe leaving her girls with Sam and Amelia.

Maybe she was overreacting to nothing. Frank and Stella had nothing to do with Adam's death. And she had nothing to do with their deaths.

She didn't feel endangered and she wasn't sure why Sam felt the need for her to have that stupid gun.

She thought better of it. Sam was a lawyer. His job was to question everything and to be a bit skeptical until he had the right answers. He didn't have those yet.

"Are you going to eat? Or better yet, talk during this meal?"

She looked up from her French toast and smiled. She hadn't eaten any of it and he'd cleaned his plate. "Sorry. I'm thinking too much about Stella and Frank."

Clayton set his fork down and reached for her hand. "Do you want to go out to Florida and see what we can do? Dorothy is here. I can use her as much as I need to."

Vivian smiled. "No. I don't want to do that. I need to let the police do what they're going to do and I'll make sure they are laid to rest respectfully."

"If you change your mind…"

She shook her head. She wouldn't change her mind.

He gave her hand a squeeze, then picked up his coffee and took a sip.

Vivian sat and admired him. His sandy hair was tussled and he hadn't shaved in two days since he'd had time off and yet he was absolutely gorgeous. There was no need to ever wonder *what if they'd met years ago.* Circumstances brought them to where they were, but she couldn't help but wonder if she could have been this happy years ago.

When the waitress brought the check, Clayton pulled dollars from his pocket and set them on the table. He then pulled a quarter from his pocket.

"Game on," he said as he flipped the coin in the air, caught it, and covered it on the back of his hand. "Heads we go right. Tails we go left."

She smiled. "Okay, let's go."

As they stepped out the door they both looked left and right.

"Left, there is a book store. Right, it looks like the court house across the street and down the street maybe a museum or something," he said.

She looked at him. "What did the coin land on?"

"Heads. So we go right."

She laughed. "Of course it did. There is a book store over here," she said pointing left. "What good is a court house on a vacation?"

But Clayton didn't laugh. In fact, his eyes widened and his face grew very serious.

"We said no plans."

She nodded. "Right."

"Because we play by all the rules."

"Yes," she drew the word out slowly.

He ran his hand over his unshaven jaw. "Everyone expects us to do everything by the book—always."

"You're starting to freak me out."

Now he laughed. "No. I don't mean to. Hear me out."

He paced in a small square in front of her.

"What's the most spontaneous thing you've ever done in your life?"

She thought for a moment. "Honestly, it was kissing you."

He smiled at that. "Ditto."

"You want to kiss me here?"

"More than you know. But…" He stopped in front of her, took her hands in his, and got down on one knee. "I know what to do in the court house."

She'd stopped breathing. She'd stopped blinking. Clayton finally stood back up and placed his hands on her shoulders.

"I didn't even say anything."

"You did. I know what you meant. You want to get married?"

His smile was back. "Yes."

"Oh, I don't…"

"Unplanned."

"But the girls…"

"We can let them dress up for a reception or something. They wanted us married."

"They want a brother."

He nodded as he let his hands slide from her shoulders to her hands. "I know."

"Oh, I don't know."

"Listen, I wouldn't do this if I didn't think someday I'd do it anyway. And Amelia and Penelope both ran off and got married after only a few weeks of knowing Adam. Now they're going to get married again. You and I've known each other a few months now. Let's get married first."

"I don't know."

His eyes lost their gleam. "If you don't want to, I understand."

VIVIAN

"It's not that I don't want to." She thought a moment about it. "You know what it is?"

He shook his head.

"It's not planned."

"That was some of the point. Not all of it, but…"

"No. I mean people wouldn't expect it. That freaks me out."

"Then forget I said it."

"No. Let's do it. I don't want to be that person anymore. I want to feel life. I want to know that I could do the craziest thing on a whim."

The corner of his mouth turned up into a smile. "You think this is crazy?"

"Yes. And I want to marry you." She began to feel the giddy tingle build inside of her. "I want to marry you now."

"You'll marry me?"

"I'll marry you."

"I'm heading right. The coin said so."

"Who am I to argue with logic like that?"

Chapter Eighteen

Two hours after walking into the courthouse and getting an open time slot to get married, Clayton was having Vivian browse rings at a small jewelry store a few blocks away.

"I don't know what I want," she said browsing bridal sets.

One thing she didn't know about her husband was what kind of disposable income he had for such things. She would imagine he didn't have any, yet here he was saying, "Choose anything."

She looked at big stones, little stone, and colored stones. She tried on high-end rings and small ones that her mother would have called *canhardlies,* as in you could hardly see a stone.

The very last set she looked at was a his –and- hers set. Matching gold bands with the woman's being thinner.

"That's it. That's what I want."

"Gold bands?"

She looked up at him and he was smiling. "Yes. Is that okay?"

He pulled her into his arms. "I mean this as an absolute compliment. One of the things I like best about you, Mrs. North, is you're a no frills kind of girl."

"You're right, I'm not."

He pressed a kiss to her lips and bought her the simple set of gold bands.

Clayton figured if they had set out to have an unexpected day they had certainly succeeded. He hadn't woken up that morning thinking that by the end of the day he'd be married. But he was—and he couldn't have been happier.

He was finding immense joy in watching her look down at the gold band he'd put on her finger. She gazed at it as other women would gaze at a gaudy diamond. But not his wife. She liked simple and he loved that.

His wife.

He loved the very sound of it in his head. Never did he think he'd remarry, but for the first time in two years he felt absolutely whole.

A part of him wanted to call their date night short and go home to tell the girls that they were in fact sisters. The very thought made him chuckle.

Vivian turned her head to him. "Why are you laughing?"

He took her hand and interlaced their fingers. "I can't wait to tell the girls that they are sisters."

She rested her head against the back of the seat. "They are going to be so happy."

He contemplated the question to her. "Do we go to them or continue on with our evening?"

Clayton caught her smile. "Don't think I'm some kind of slut, but I don't think I can hold out much longer."

"I would never think that of you." He gave her hand a squeeze. "I'm feeling the exact same way."

He wasn't one to speed, but he was sure he'd have gotten a ticket as he pulled up in front of the old house.

He turned off the car. "I don't think I've ever been so glad to know a house was empty."

Vivian tucked her lips between her teeth. "I'll bet sometime from sixteen through nineteen you were glad."

VIVIAN

He laughed easily as he lifted her hand to his lips and kissed her fingers. "You're right. But as a grown adult—I'm pretty happy."

"Me too." She flung open her door. "Let's go."

Clayton pushed open his door and stepped out into the street. "Grab your bag. I don't want to have to come out here for anything."

She laughed as she grabbed her bag and then ran to the front door to open it.

With the key in her hand she pushed open the door, dropped her bag on the ground, and waited for Clayton to follow. She quickly pushed it shut and locked it before she found herself pushed up against it.

Clayton's mouth was hot on hers as he pushed his body hard to hers. Her breath came out in a moan against his mouth.

Her heart beat an erratic rhythm against his as his hands slid over the curve of her bottom, pulling her even closer—if possible.

Vivian tangled her fingers into his hair. How could she have forgotten how amazing it felt to have a man pressed to her with his desire evident in his touch and constricted by his clothing?

He moved his hands to the buttons on her shirt, making quick work to expose her beneath.

Clayton lifted his head to look at her and a deep growl came from his throat as he moved his lips down her neck toward her breasts that heaved beneath his lips.

She closed her eyes and allowed herself to breathe in the moment. As he cupped her in his hands and exposed her delicate skin beneath the pads of his fingers, she let out a hum of delight.

"You're beautiful, Vivian."

"You're going to kill me with all of this attention."

He raised back to her lips and took her mouth. "I plan to pay a lot of attention to each part of you—forever."

She swallowed hard. "Take me upstairs before I lose my mind."

~*~

The air had swirled between them for nearly the past two hours as Clayton and his new wife explored this very personal part of their marriage.

Passion like nothing Clayton had ever felt burned inside of him as he rolled from atop of his new wife who still gasped for air.

He looked over at her sweat slickened body, appreciating every curve of her. The marks that marred her skin from the birth of her daughters only made her more precious to him.

"I'm glad we waited for that," Vivian said on a sated breath.

"I can't believe we did." He rolled to his side and brushed a strand of her hair aside. "We're going to have to learn to be more quiet."

She laughed and her white teeth shined in the dim room. "I promise." She turned to look at him. "What time is it?"

"Dark."

She laughed again and he realized he could just get drunk on the sound of it.

"Is it bad that I want to tell my girls goodnight?"

"No. C'mon, let's go down and find something to eat. I could use some water."

VIVIAN

He walked into the bathroom and pulled down a towel, wrapping it around his waist as she pulled the sheet off the bed.

The house was eerily dark he thought. They would need some motion lights when they moved in—and a gate at the top of the stairs.

"I'll go get our bags and our phones," he said giving her rear a pat.

He could hear the refrigerator open as he moved toward the front door. Noticing the front porch light was turned off, he flicked the switch to turn it on. He knew Sam had put it on a sensor. Maybe it had stopped working. He'd have to look at it tomorrow.

As he picked up his bag he noticed the door wasn't locked. He was sure they'd done that too. They must have been in one hell of a hurry to leave the door unlocked.

With a flick of his fingers he secured the deadbolt and headed back to the kitchen with their bags.

Outside the wind began to blow and he could see the now bare trees sway in the moonlight outside the kitchen window.

"I found chicken nuggets," Vivian said with a smile.

"I don't even care at this point. I haven't eaten since breakfast and we certainly wore that off."

He watched her load up a plate of the frozen clumps and put them in the microwave. Picking up his phone he called his house.

"Hey Dorothy."

"How is your evening?" she asked and he could only smile, looking at his wife in a bed sheet cooking chicken nuggets.

"It's amazing. How are the girls?"

"Asleep on the floor. I told them we'd have a slumber party in the front room."

He laughed. "I'll bet they're loving having you there."

"Well, I've decided they'll get to do this any time. I'm going to stay, Clayton. If you were serious about me living here."

"I am." He wanted to tell her about what they'd done today, but the girls needed to be the first ones to hear it. "I just called to say goodnight, but I'll let them sleep. Thank you for taking them."

"My pleasure. Enjoy yourself," she said and his heart raced just a bit faster. He hadn't thought about Linda much all day, until that moment. But it didn't hurt for the first time.

"We will." He disconnected the phone and looked at Vivian. "Mine are asleep.

"Let me call mine." She reached for her phone.

"We forgot to lock the door when we raced upstairs," he said, giving the sheet around her a yank.

Her eyes fixed on his. "No. I locked it."

He shrugged. "Maybe we jostled it."

She looked at her phone. There was a text from Sam. *Stay there. I'm coming over.*

"Why did he send me this?" She showed Clayton the text.

"If he's coming over we'd better get dressed," Clayton joked just as they heard something crash upstairs. "What the hell?"

He looked back outside and the wind had kicked up.

"Maybe something blew over in the attic. We have those walls torn out."

Vivian watched him readjust his towel.

VIVIAN

"I'll go up with you."

He gave her a smile and touched her face. "Are you afraid of something?"

"No, just…" She didn't know. She just couldn't stand to be away from him for even a moment. "I'm coming with you."

They took the first few steps before her phone chimed again from the kitchen.

"It's probably Sam. Go check."

She gave him a nod and headed back to the kitchen to retrieve her phone.

Her hands began to shake as she picked up her phone and the display read MESSAGE FROM STELLA MONROE.

"Clayton! Clayton!" Her voice shook and wasn't as loud as she thought it should be.

The text came up on the screen. *Stella. Frank. Now it's his turn.*

As she took a breath to yell his name again, she heard the horrid sound of something being hit and then falling down the steps of the attic.

"Clayton!"

Dropping her phone, she went for her bag. Fumbling with the zipper, she finally managed it open and grabbed for the gun Sam had given her.

She pulled it back to cock it and it shook in her hands. Wrapping the other hand around the handle she called out again, "Clayton!"

There wasn't an answer. There should have been some damn answer.

With the sheet wrapped loosely around her and the gun trembling in her hands, she started up the steps.

"Clayton, c'mon. I don't like this. Where are you?"

As she crested the top of the steps, she could see the steps to the attic were down. Another two steps, she could see Clayton on the ground face down at the bottom of the steps.

Her first reaction was to run right to him. The back of his head was covered in blood and a baseball bat was lying next to him covered in blood.

"Clayton! Oh, God!" She set the gun on the ground in front of her. "Clayton, please wake up. Please!"

She pressed her fingers to his neck, but she wasn't sure if she felt anything. Her fingers were covered in his blood. The only thing she could hear was her heart beating in her ears.

Her head spun and her eyes filled with tears blinding her from the shadow that moved across the attic. A moment later, someone flew at her, knocking her back on her back, her head slamming into the floor.

She struggled beneath the gangly limbs of a man who held her hands to the ground.

"You're going to work harder than that," the man said as he dipped his head to her collarbone and bit down.

Vivian screamed. "Get off me! Get off!"

"My turn."

And as the man pushed up the sheet she'd had wrapped around her she managed her knee between his thighs just enough to have him roll off of her.

"Bitch!" He yelled as she rolled toward the gun she'd laid next to Clayton.

The sheet tangled around her, but she fought to grasp the gun as he came back toward her and the moonlight caught his face.

"Darby!"

VIVIAN

"Give me the damn gun, Vivian." He lurched toward her knocking her back again and ripping the gun from her hand. "You're so weak!"

"Darby! Get off of me!" She fought him. "What are you doing?"

He kept his body on her legs and her arms pinned with his. In his right hand, he held the gun he'd ripped from her and it pressed into her skin as he held her against the wall.

"Where do I begin?" He pressed the metal of the gun further into her skin. "First, Adam took you from me."

"Darby, that was a long time ago. Please," she pleaded. "I have to get him some help." She was looking toward Clayton.

"C'mon, let's just take care of this now." He took the gun and pointed it toward Clayton.

"No!" She screamed and lurched to try and reach the gun, but he only came back with it and smacked her in the head with it.

Now her vision was slipping away with her consciousness.

"You'll die here with him." She could feel his breath on her face and his hands on her bare thighs. "I want the money, Vivian. Where is all the money?"

He squeezed her thigh and the pain shot through her, but she couldn't move. She couldn't see. It was getting harder to even breathe.

"She hid all the money in this house, Vivian. I know she did."

"Don't—have," she managed and he squeezed her thigh higher and tighter.

"You know why I hated Adam as much as I did?" His mouth was on her again, pressed now to her ear. "It was my father Stella Monroe had an affair with. That's right. My bastard father left my pregnant mother for a married woman. Her nasty spawn was Adam."

He moved his knee into her groin and she cried out.

"Let me go. I'll get the money for you."

She felt his hands on her hips and her body was yanked from the wall and slammed down to the floor again. He held the gun under her chin and pushed up the sheet.

"He took you. He got you. I'm done being the forgotten one."

He straddled her, then sat up, but she couldn't see now. Her eyes had swollen nearly shut.

She knew he'd sat up and then another shadow moved across them and Darby had been knocked to the ground. A white light exploded in the darkness with the crack of a gun.

Chapter Nineteen

Vivian had heard the scream and she knew it was her own, but she couldn't see. She couldn't feel.

Another set of hands were on her and she screamed again.

"Vivian, it's Sam. Honey, calm down."

She scrambled toward him, wrapping her arms around his neck.

"The ambulance and police are coming."

She couldn't let go. Her body shook and she could feel the cold of the air around them, which meant the sheet had fallen away.

"Darby! Darby! He killed Clayton. Darby…" she kept repeating.

Sam took her hands. "Clayton's alive. But we have to get him to the hospital. You too."

"Darby," she said his name quietly now.

"I didn't kill him. I want him to pay for what he's done."

"Stella. Frank."

"I know." He pulled her toward him as the flashing lights from outside illuminated the house.

Vivian watched them load Clayton into the ambulance. He was still unresponsive, but he was alive. She had to focus on that.

She held an icepack to her face as she sat on the sidewalk wrapped now in a robe and a blanket.

Amelia appeared from around the ambulance they'd loaded Darby into. She was running and crying as she fell down next to Vivian.

"God, look at you. Oh, God!" She pulled her into her arms.

It was time to let the pain out and she began to sob against Amelia.

"Darby. It was Darby."

"I know. Oh, honey, I know." She rocked her back and forth.

Vivian pulled back. "My girls. Where are my girls?"

Amelia pulled her back to her. "With Dorothy."

The paramedic moved toward them. "Ma'am, we're ready to transport your husband. Will you be riding with us?"

Vivian nodded and Amelia helped her to her feet.

"I'll get you some clothes," she said as Vivian walked toward the ambulance.

"Thank you."

She held out her hand to the paramedic to help her inside.

"Wait!" Amelia moved toward the ambulance. "Husband?"

Vivian held up her hand as they closed the doors between them.

~*~

Clayton woke with a splitting headache. He had to force himself to open his eyes.

The room was dimly lit and unfamiliar.

He tried to sit up, but the pain in his head was so immense he only closed his eyes again.

"Clayton?"

The angelic voice was one he recognized. Again, he forced himself to open his eyes.

VIVIAN

Standing next to him was a vision—a glorious vision. His beautiful wife.

"Vivian, what happened to you?"

She raised her hand to her cheek. "Darby."

"What did he do to you?" His eyes had managed to open wider to take in the bruises on her face and her neck. "Jesus, what is that?" He tried to reach for the mark on her collarbone, but she winced away.

"Nothing. Don't move."

"I don't remember anything. I walked up the stairs, that's all I remember."

"Darby hit you with a bat. You have a head full of stitches."

"Ah, that would explain this headache I have."

She smiled at his joke, no matter how weak it was.

"They'll give you some more medicine. The nurse said they would."

Clayton reached for her hand. "Some honeymoon, huh?"

"I thought you died," the tears in her voice made him ache even more than he already was.

"I wouldn't leave you that easily." He gave her hand a squeeze. "Where is he?"

"Sam shot him."

He sucked in a deep breath. "Dead?"

Vivian shook her head. "No. He wants him to pay for what he did."

"Frank and Stella?"

She nodded and then moved to sit on the edge of the bed. "Dorothy told the girls you fell down and you are in the hospital."

"She's quick on her feet."

"She's worried about you. You're her child too, you know."

He managed a smile. "I do know." He twisted her gold band between his fingers. "Did you tell her?"

"No. Only Amelia. Which means that Sam might know."

"Everyone will know as soon as the girls know."

She nodded. "They want to keep you for a few more hours."

"Doesn't a bed in a hospital come with Jell-O?"

"I'll go find you some," she said standing.

"Mrs. North," he called as she moved from the bed and she turned back toward him. "I love you."

"I love you too."

Vivian stepped out into the hall. As soon as the door to his room closed she leaned against the wall and let the tears she'd been holding on to fall.

When they told her that Adam had died she got mad. The tears hadn't come for days. But the moment she'd seen Clayton laying on the ground, everything inside of her wanted to release.

She had to remind herself that he was alive and he was fine. He'd been making jokes and keeping her comfortable.

She wrapped her arms around herself.

"Mrs. North," someone called.

She lifted her head to see Sam walking toward her.

"I thought that might be the case," he joked as he moved closer to her and pulled her into his arms. "Are you okay?"

"I thought he was dead."

VIVIAN

"I wish I'd have been five minutes faster," he said, stroking her hair. "He'd texted me. I just didn't know you two would be there, well…"

She slapped his arm, then pulled back and looked at him. "Thank you. If you hadn't come…"

"I did. This is over."

She nodded. "He wants Jell-O."

"He's going to have to wait. There is someone here looking for you."

"For me?"

A smile formed on Sam's face. "Penelope is in labor. She wants to see you."

Vivian's heart began to race again.

Penelope was having her baby—Adam's baby.

Vivian took a deep breath. She had to be supportive. She had to be ready.

For the past six months they'd all moved past their failed marriages to Adam, but he was still very much around. He was in her girls and in Penelope's baby. Without Adam hiring Sam, Amelia wouldn't have fallen in love. Had he not sent Brock, Penelope wouldn't have anyone but Vivian and Amelia to love her and her baby. And though he hadn't hand delivered Clayton to her door, without months of learning who she was and who she could be—she wouldn't have fallen in love again.

"Where is she?" She asked.

"C'mon, I'll take you down."

Sam escorted her to Penelope's room.

She was seated on the bed with the back raised and her hands rested on her stomach as she breathed in short pants.

"Oh, what happened to you?" Penelope winced as a contraction obviously moved through her.

"Just a little run in with Darby. I'm fine." She moved toward the bed. "Are you ready?"

Penelope nodded. "But I had to apologize first."

"For what?" Vivian's voice rose as she couldn't think of one thing for the woman to apologize about, especially while she was in labor.

"For marrying your husband. I'm sorry."

Vivian smiled and held her hand. "Without Adam's misunderstandings of *everything*, we wouldn't have each other."

"You forgive me?"

Vivian shook her head and her heart nearly exploded with love for the girl who had sweat beading on her lip. "I forgive him."

Amelia moved in next to her. "I think they're ready for you to do this."

"I don't know. I'm scared."

They both took Penelope's hand. "We're a team," Vivian said. "Remember?"

"If we were a team you'd have invited us to your wedding," Amelia jabbed an elbow into Vivian's side.

"You're married?" Penelope's eyes opened wide as much for the contraction she was having as the news of Vivian's marriage.

She jabbed back at Amelia. "Why do you have to ruin surprises? Did you tell her you're pregnant too?"

Penelope grit her teeth. "You're pregnant?"

Amelia jabbed back at Vivian. "I said to not say anything until the wedding."

"Ahhhh!" Penelope held tight to her stomach. "The baby is coming. The baby is coming and you two are married, pregnant, and still fighting." She grimaced at the

VIVIAN

pain and Brock moved in closer to her. "Go get those girls of yours. They're about to meet their sibling."

Vivian and Amelia both watched as they readied her for the birth of Adam's baby.

Vivian looked up at Brock. "Thank you for taking care of her."

His eyes were wide with the anticipation of what was about to happen, but he smiled sweetly. "I love her."

Vivian and Amelia walked out of the room with their arms wrapped around each other. Who would have ever thought they'd be kindred souls?

"I suppose I should call Dorothy," Vivian said as they waked toward the waiting room.

"I did."

As they turned the corner Vivian smiled at the room full of people there.

All of Brock's family sat in the room. His mother and father entertained his nieces and nephews. His brother's wife sat rubbing her own growing stomach while his sister read a book to one of her children. Dorothy sat with the four girls lined up next to her. Weren't they a sight?

Amelia nudged her again. "You should take them to see their daddy."

Vivian nodded. "You're right."

She walked across the room toward Dorothy whose eyes opened wide the moment she looked at her.

"Were you in an accident?"

Vivian rested her hand on Dorothy's. "Sort of." She looked at the girls who now looked up at her. She knelt down in front of Charlotte and Stephanie. "I want to take you to see your daddy. He's in a room here. We did kinda get into an accident and he's got some stitches in the back of his head," she said as she pointed to where his injuries would be. "He has a big bandage on his head, but I know if he saw you girls it would make him feel better."

They looked at her and she knew she must be a horrible mess with her blackened eyes, swollen cheek, and the deep mark on her collarbone where Darby had bit her.

"I'm okay. And so is your daddy."

Emma tugged on her shirt. "Can we go with you?"

Vivian pulled her close to her and kissed the top of her head. "Yes. We want to talk to all of you." She looked at Dorothy. "Please come too."

Her girls took her hands and Clayton's girls each held Dorothy's. Quietly they walked down the hall toward the room where Clayton rested.

Vivian poked her head in the door. "Hey, I have some people here to see you."

His eyes widened and a smile formed on his lips as if he knew who was beyond the door.

"Bring them in."

The four girls walked into the room slowly. Emma and Ava stood close to their mother. Stephanie stared at her father, but Charlotte moved right to his bed.

"You fall?" she asked as she looked at the marks on his face.

"I did. I fell down the attic stairs," he said and Vivian knew that was still the truth and he was okay telling her that. "Do I scare you?"

Charlotte shook her head, but Stephanie stood pressing her body into Dorothy.

"It's okay. I'm going to get to come home tonight and I'll be better soon. So will Vivian."

VIVIAN

"I have some essential oils that'll help all that bruising you both have," Dorothy said and then raised an eyebrow. "I'm sure you'll explain that *fall* as soon as we get home."

Clayton smiled. "Of course we will." He looked at all of the girls and then to Vivian.

She smiled at him, genuinely happy about what they were about to tell the girls. "Clayton and I want to tell you something." She looked up at Dorothy. "All of you."

He reached for her hand and she moved closer to him, both girls still clinging tightly to her.

"Yesterday I took your mommy on a long date," he said to her girls as he gave her hand a squeeze. "I asked her to marry me."

Emma and Ava exchanged looks. "Is she going to marry you?" Emma asked.

"She said she would."

They exchanged looks again and then looked toward the other two. "So we will be sisters?"

"Is that okay with you?"

Charlotte began to jump up and down. "Sisters."

"Well, here's the deal." He gazed up at Vivian. "You are all sisters now. We got married yesterday."

The girls jumped up and down and squealed in delight. But when Vivian looked toward Dorothy she was batting back tears with her hand over her mouth.

Vivian went to her. "I'm sorry. This wasn't meant to upset you."

She waved off the apology. "I'm not upset. I look at him and I know he loves you. Oh, I'll never let her go. But I'll never let him go either and I want him happy."

"I do too," Vivian added as Dorothy pulled her into an embrace.

There was a tapping at the door and Amelia stuck her head in. "She's here," she said with a soft voice and a wide smile.

"She?"

"She."

Vivian wanted to hate this moment, but she couldn't. She was absolutely giddy at the thought of seeing Penelope's baby—Adam's baby.

"I'll be right down." She looked at Clayton and then at Emma and Ava. "It's a busy day for you. In one day you each went from having one sister to having four."

Emma scrunched up her face. "Four?"

Vivian crouched down and held them both at arm's length. "Penelope just had a baby girl. You have a new sister."

Their eyes went wide and this time Ava jumped up and down, but Emma looked at her, her face pinched in thought.

"So I got my sister from Penelope. When do I get my brother?"

Vivian pulled her in tightly. "We will talk about that, okay?"

Emma nodded. "Can we see her?"

"I'm sure you'll be able to in a little bit. You stay here with Dorothy and…"

"Grandma Dorothy," she said looking at Ava and Emma and then up at Vivian. "It's Grandma."

Vivian's lip began to tremble. "Grandma Dorothy." She let out a sigh. How could she be so thankful at that moment to her late husband and love Clayton's late wife and her family so much?

VIVIAN

She took a moment to cleanse her mind before looking at the girls again. "You stay with Grandma Dorothy and I'll go check and see when you can visit the baby."

They nodded in agreement and then occupied themselves with their other sisters trying to amuse Clayton.

As Vivian passed by Dorothy she reached out her hand and touched her arm. "Thank you. Thank you for everything."

Dorothy patted her hand and looked in Clayton's direction. "You saved him and not just last night."

Her heart was full and her body warm. This was the kind of love she'd been searching for years.

Chapter Twenty

Amelia was in the hallway when Vivian stepped out of Clayton's room.

"Are they excited for a baby sister?" she asked.

Vivian laughed. "Oh sure. And they want a baby brother."

"My baby doesn't count. He wouldn't be their brother."

Vivian wrapped her arm around Amelia. "He'd be pretty close. But I told them we'd talk about it."

They walked back toward Penelope's room and tapped on the door. Brock invited them in and they stepped in just far enough to see Penelope holding her baby draped in a pink blanket.

"Come here. Come see her," she urged them in a hoarse, tired voice.

Vivian and Amelia walked toward her with their arms linked and looked down at the beautiful little bundle.

"Oh, Penelope," Vivian's voice cracked. "She's beautiful."

"I think she looks like Ava. Don't you?"

Vivian nodded. "I do. Ava looks the most like Adam."

"I thought so too," Penelope said softly.

Amelia lowered her head toward her, but didn't reach out to touch. "What's her name?"

Penelope looked up at Brock who moved in next to her. "Gwendolyn Monroe Romero."

Vivian felt the tears sting in her throat. "I like it. It's a beautiful name."

Brock smoothed his hand over the top of the baby's head. "We wanted Adam to always be part of her. Without him we wouldn't have each other."

VIVIAN

Penelope looked up at Vivian and Amelia. "And we wouldn't have each other either."

Vivian let out a chuckle. "I just realized it's Thanksgiving."

"You're right," Amelia said. "You two ruined Thanksgiving."

Vivian shook her head and laughed. "It's been a long time since I was thankful for anything. I think that's all changed."

Penelope looked up at the both of them, then focused on Vivian. "Did you really get married last night?"

Brock's head snapped up and Vivian only smiled.

"I've never done anything so spur of the moment in my life." She looked at them both. "Don't criticize. You both ran off and married my husband. I deserve the right to run off and get married to someone I just met too. And now I'm married before both of you."

"You make everything into a contest don't you?" Amelia scoffed.

"Me? That would be you. I…"

"Shhhh," Penelope scolded. "She's sleeping and you both always argue."

"We do not," Amelia whispered.

"Yeah," Vivian added with a smile.

Penelope kissed her daughter's forehead before she looked back up at Amelia.

"Are you really having a baby?"

Amelia gave a shrug. "Yes, that's what the stick said. And then the doctor said."

"I think you'll be a good mom," Penelope said softly and Vivian let out a cough.

"She's going to be extremely overwhelmed."

"What if I'm a perfect mother?" Amelia fisted her hands on her hips. "I might be better than you are."

"At least I'll be around to see. Then I'll laugh. And then I can save you if you need it."

Amelia just laughed and Vivian knew they'd all be around for when the other one needed them.

"The girls want to see their sister. Are you ready for them or do you need a few moments?" Vivian asked, as the moment grew serious again.

"Bring them in. I want them to see her before anyone else. Adam's girls."

When she said that, Vivian looked up at Brock to see his reaction, but he was gazing down at Penelope and the baby. He wasn't worried about Gwendolyn Monroe being Adam's girl. He was obviously confident enough to know she'd always be his little girl.

Vivian walked back through the door a few minutes later with Emma and Ava, each holding one of her hands. She wondered if they'd sleep at all tonight. They had to be very overwhelmed. Their mother looked like she'd slammed her face into the ground. Their stepfather, which they just found out they had, looked just as bad. They'd found out their new best-friends were their sisters and their actual sister was born. Even Vivian wasn't sure she could wrap her head around it.

"Hi, girls," Penelope said very softly. "Do you want to meet your sister?"

Both girls nodded, but neither of them made a move toward her bed until Vivian gave them a little push.

"Isn't she beautiful?" Vivian asked and two little heads nodded in unison.

"I thought she'd be bigger," Emma said.

VIVIAN

"She will be soon," Vivian assured her. "You can get a little closer."

Ava was the first to reach for her little hand. Gwendolyn quickly wrapped her hand around Ava's little finger and she giggled.

"She hold me."

"She sure did."

Vivian hadn't been prepared for the feelings that would wash over her as the girls gazed at their sister. She remembered those moments, lying in a hospital bed holding her girls. There was an overwhelming sense of pride and accomplishment. There was a love that enlarged her heart.

Watching Brock stroke Penelope's hair and kiss Gwendolyn's head made her heart ache. Adam hadn't been there to share that moment with her. Sam would share it with Amelia. And she knew, without even having to ask, that Clayton had shared those moments with Linda.

Amelia stepped in and wrapped her arm around Vivian. "Are you okay?"

"I'm having a moment."

"You'll have another chance."

Vivian looked up at her. "For what?"

"You and Clayton can have more babies."

Vivian shook her head. "How did you know that was what I was thinking about?"

"I've learned a lot about you in the past six months."

"I've learned a lot about me too." She rested her head on Amelia's shoulder. "But we now have four girls all about the same age. I don't see us having any more kids. This is just going to have to be something I miss out on."

Amelia gave her a little squeeze.

"I wanna howd her," Ava turned to Vivian.

"Oh, I don't…"

"I'd love to have her hold her," Penelope said. "This is her sister. I want them to love her and of course we need some pictures of them. Gwendolyn will want pictures of this for her scrapbook."

Vivian smiled. "I think that's precious." She looked at Ava and Emma. "First things first. We need to wash our hands and then find a nice big chair to sit in."

Both girls' eyes opened wide. "Why do I have to wash my hands?" Emma asked in protest.

"I said so, mainly. But Gwendolyn is only a few minutes old. She needs you to be clean. You'll have lots of time in your life to get her dirty."

That had caused Penelope to laugh and Amelia followed. Vivian realized that she missed out on a lot of special moments in her life. But it was time to start collecting them. She'd start paying attention to everything from here on out.

~*~

Thanksgiving was held on Sunday, and Vivian thought it might just be the best Thanksgiving she'd ever had. The old house on Main and Pine was filled with family.

After the run in with Darby, her parents flew in to help with the girls. They were a little more than surprised to find out she'd met a man and married him six months after her husband had died. But she was fairly confident that when they'd met him, they too had fallen in love with him.

Charlotte and Stephanie bonded with her parents and that had filled her heart as well. Love came in so many forms. She'd fallen in love with Amelia and Penelope—which still surprised her. She loved Sam and Brock.

VIVIAN

Clayton, well she was certain that a part of her had fallen in love with him the moment he knocked on the door of the daycare center looking for care for his girls. And those girls—oh she loved them and she was thrilled that she'd get to be the one carrying on as their mother—though she'd always be clear, they had a wonderful mother. That she was sure of.

She'd fallen in love with Dorothy—Grandma Dorothy.

Knowing Dorothy had chosen to stay in Parson's Gulch had her equally as happy. Clayton needed family around, even his in-laws. But Vivian knew it would be good to have her there too. Not only had she fallen in love with her, but the girls would always have that part of their mother with them. That was invaluable.

As the families mingled and everyone took their turn to hold and love Gwendolyn, Vivian realized that she still loved the one man who'd brought them all together. Oh, it wasn't the same as what she felt for Clayton. She was crazy in love with him. But there had been a time when Adam had made her head spin with ideas of what could come. Who would have thought that what was to come would be her there holding Adam's daughter?

"You look very natural with a little baby in your arms," Clayton sat down next to her and wrapped his arm around her shoulders.

"It feels good. And she's so beautiful."

"She looks just like Ava. I'm sure they'll hear that a lot when they get older."

Vivian rested her head on his shoulder. "He would have loved her," she said, her voice cracking and a tear sliding down her cheek.

"He's where he can watch over her—all of them. Remember, he was a hero. That's what she'll know."

Oh, this man was a gem. Was there any situation he couldn't fix with just words?

Vivian looked up and spotted her mother, with Ava on her hip, looking at them smiling.

"I think my mother loves you," she said.

Clayton looked up and smiled at her. "I asked them for their blessing. I told them I realized we were already married, but their blessing would mean a lot."

"I love how you think." She pressed a kiss to his lips.

The doorbell rang and Vivian noticed that Brock quickly moved through his family to answer it. A moment later a man with a white collar walked through the door, escorted by Brock.

He pointed toward Penelope who stood slowly from her seat.

"Father Josh, this is my Penelope," he said and Vivian felt the words *my Penelope* squeeze at her heart.

Penelope shook the minister's hand before Brock took hold of both of her hands.

"I know this isn't how you'd planned for this, but Penelope, I'd like to marry you here, now, with our families surrounding us."

"Brock!" Her eyes were open wide as she scanned the room. "You planned this?"

"Last minute really. I met Father Josh at the hospital. But we are starting a new life here with Gwendolyn and my entire family is here. Will you marry me today? After all, this is our Thanksgiving and there is nothing I'm more thankful for than you and our little Gwen."

Penelope reached her hand to his cheek. "I'd love to marry you today."

"I hoped that's what you'd say."

VIVIAN

Penelope, Vivian, and Amelia sat in the bedroom they'd originally designed for Penelope and the baby. Together they'd fussed with her hair and added some makeup. Vivian wasn't sure she needed any. She still had that glow to her.

Gwendolyn slept in her infant seat after having been fed.

"I didn't think this is what I'd be doing this morning," Penelope said as she looked into the dresser mirror.

"He's right," Amelia said as she looked at her in the mirror. "What better day to get married than on a day built around thanks."

Penelope turned and looked at them both. "I've been thinking about Adam a lot the past few days. I suppose it's because of Gwendolyn." She looked down at the sleeping baby. "Am I pushing him out of my life?"

"Adam?" Vivian moved toward her.

"He's only been gone six months."

"And you only knew him a few weeks." She took Penelope's hands in hers. "What good would it be to live in mourning and not going on with what he gave you?" They all looked at the baby. "Look what he gave you."

"Are you mad at me?"

Vivian turned back to her. "For what?"

"For her?"

Vivian shook her head. "I was mad the moment I met you. I was mad the moment I found out about her. But," she let out a sigh, "I found out I loved you both as much as I ever thought I loved Adam. And I love your baby—his baby. I'm the one who is thankful that I get to be with her."

They both turned when they saw Amelia's shoulders bounce and they realized she was crying.

"Is this normal? I've been crying lately. I don't cry. I don't like crying."

Penelope nodded. "I cried the whole time."

"I know," Amelia sobbed.

Vivian could feel the rise of her own tears. "Oh, you guys are sissies." She pulled them both in and held them tight.

Vivian stood next to Amelia and Brock's sister Sadie. She gazed lovingly at her own husband Clayton who stood next to Sam and Brock's brother Mason. Gwendolyn cooed in her grandmother's arms.

Vivian had always thought Penelope was beautiful, but watching her walk down the stairs toward Brock—well she'd never seen anyone look so amazing.

The ceremony in the toddler room was quick, but lovely and Amelia cried the entire time.

Sam wrapped her in his arms. "I never thought I'd see this side of you."

"They assure me I'll be doing it a lot."

"I think the reason behind your emotional breakdowns is the best reason to be crying."

She gave him a shove.

"Okay, there's my girl."

That made her laugh as she rested her head on his shoulder again.

Mason and Sadie walked into the room each with a tray of champagne flutes. "Okay, Sadie has the wussy stuff for pregnant and nursing mothers. And the yummy stuff," he lowered his voice to be deeper, "for the four young ladies who are sisters."

They giggled and headed toward Sadie to take their drinks in the fancy glasses.

Everyone in the room was handed a flute and they raised them toward the bride and groom.

VIVIAN

"To the married couple."

Each of them sipped and Amelia, Vivian, and Penelope settled their eyes on one another.

They took one another's hands and walked out onto the front porch of the house that Frank Monroe had given them and looked up toward the starry sky above.

"I never thought that I'd say this, but Adam Monroe, this is for you," Amelia raised her glass to the sky.

"To Adam," Penelope raised her glass.

Vivian raised her glass up toward the stars. "To Adam Monroe." She let out a sigh and smiled. "Thank you."

Each of them sipped from their glass and Vivian turned to see Clayton and their four girls looking out the window at her. She gave him a smile and he blew her a kiss.

God, she was Happy.

Epilogue

July in Parson's Gulch, Oklahoma was never bearable. But for a pregnant woman, it was worse. Vivian was just glad she was in the early stages, because Amelia looked miserable.

The headstones for Frank and Stella Monroe had turned out nicer than Vivian could have ever expected. She laid the bouquet of flowers she'd brought for them on their grave.

Darby had been indicted in the deaths of Frank and Stella. He'd been harboring that hate in him for a long time. Vivian wondered how he'd never let it slip, in all those years, that Adam was his brother.

He'd been to the house on Main Street and Pine dozens of times, he'd confessed in court. It just happened that one night they'd finally caught him, as he'd run out of the house after texting Vivian from Stella's stolen phone.

She and Clayton had moved into the house right before Christmas. Brock had been a genius on remodeling the bedroom and the attic. The girls had loved it. It was nice too when she could just walk downstairs and be at work in the daycare center they'd opened.

And wasn't it interesting that in the many boxes stored away in the attic they'd found the original wedding license for her marriage to Adam? Now that she knew Stella's medical conditions, only enhanced by her drinking, it was no wonder it had been lost for so many years.

As they walked toward Adam's grave, each with a bouquet of flowers, Amelia stopped and stretched her back.

"I don't ever want to do this again," she moaned.

VIVIAN

"You will, trust me." Penelope said rubbing her unswollen, yet pregnant belly.

"You're crazy," Amelia said. "You're going to have two babies under two."

She smiled at her. "It's called a blessing."

Amelia shook her head. "Then Vivian is crazy blessed. She has four girls under five and now she's having a little boy to throw into the mix."

Vivian only smiled. "Finally, a little boy. He's in for it, isn't he?"

"He'll be fine. I can handle little boys. Think of the things I can teach your son." Amelia grinned as they approached Adam's grave.

Looking at Adam's name on that stone never got easier, Vivian thought. In the past six months she'd been to his grave at least every month to talk to him about his girls—all of them. Marrying Clayton had brought her peace and she was able to embrace the love and life she'd had with Adam Monroe.

Each of them took a step forward, lay down their bouquet, and then stepped back. It was quiet now, as they reflected.

It had been a year since he'd saved the many lives he'd saved, including Brock's. It had been a year since they'd said goodbye to him and met each other.

They'd grown as individuals in that year. They'd met in anger and turmoil only to learn to respect, forgive, and love. Vivian thought of these women at her side as her sisters. She owed Adam for that, in the strange way it came to be. That's why she'd come each month too and talked to him and Clayton encouraged her to do so.

Together, today on the anniversary of Adam's death, Mrs. Jackson, Mrs. Romero, and Mrs. North came to pay their respects to a man they'd all loved, whom they'd all married, and now they all understood. Because of the many secrets Adam Monroe kept, without even knowing it, he'd brought together these three women who were now family and had once all been one of the three Mrs. Monroes.

We hope you enjoyed the conclusion of
The Three Mrs. Monroes

Please enjoy an excerpt from another bestselling trilogy by
Bernadette Marie

MATCHMAKERS

MATCHMAKERS ~ CHAPTER ONE

Sophia filed off the airplane along with the other groggy passengers. The red-eye flight to Kansas City had knotted up her stomach. What in the hell was she doing back here?

Perfect persuasion and just the right amount of guilt had gotten her on that plane. Perhaps the tightening of her stomach wasn't the flying—it could very well be that she'd returned to the very place she'd run from ten years ago.

She'd run from a man and shattered the hearts of people she loved. The guilt stung a little deeper. She should have come home years earlier.

Sophia followed a small group of women from the plane into the ladies' room. Exhaustion weighed down her shoulders. Within the hour, she'd be at her grandmother's house, tucked into her childhood bed, and asleep. In the meantime, she splashed cool water on her face to keep herself alert.

She dried her face and hands and adjusted the scarf at her neck to ensure it hid the secret she kept from the world. She picked up the carry-on luggage at her feet and headed toward baggage claim.

"Sophia."

The husky voice was soft and male and made her knees weak when she heard it. She knew that voice as well as she knew her own. The knot in her stomach returned, but this time it was like a fist in her gut.

She turned to see him standing there in his pilot's uniform with his suitcase at his side—David Kendal, the very man she'd run from so many years ago.

He took his pilot's hat off and revealed the dark, wavy

hair that she'd once run her fingers through. It was now speckled with hints of sophisticated silver. His uniform was striking on him—just as it had always been. Even in the early morning hour, she felt her skin tingle when she looked at his broad shoulders and knew what it was like to rest her head against his chest.

"David." His name floated from her lips in a sigh. Ten years had passed since she'd last laid eyes on him, and now he was as large as life standing before her.

"I thought that was you on the plane." He was walking closer to her, and her trembling knees wouldn't allow her to run the other direction.

The scent of his cologne washed over her. His dark eyes were smoky and wide as she watched him take in the sight of her.

"You look wonderful." He stepped closer, and Sophia gripped her bag tighter and tried to swallow the ball of fear that had lodged in her throat. He gripped his hat tighter. "I've been following your career."

"Really?" The muscles in her shoulders tensed. "Why?"

"Why?" He chuckled and took one more step closer, and her throat constricted. "Sophia, you're…" He shrugged as though brushing off a thought. "You're very talented."

Sophia shook her head, trying desperately to remove all thoughts of him from before—of what she'd lost. She sighed. "David, it was nice to see you. I really need to get my luggage."

She turned from him, head up, shoulders back, and strode toward the elevator, stepping in as the door closed. She leaned her head against the back wall and closed her eyes.

How was it possible that after ten years he could stir such feelings in her? Sophia took inventory of what she was feeling. There was a surge of attraction between them. Then the anger she'd felt for years accompanied the thought of him. She'd walked out on him. His betrayal was much stronger than the attraction. It had given her purpose to make something of herself. Her success as a concert cellist sprang as much from her desire to succeed as it did from a need to escape her feelings for David.

Sophia opened her eyes when she heard the elevator doors open. The small group of others who had been aboard the plane with her stood watching the empty luggage carousel go around. Sophia waited for her cello case to arrive in the oversized luggage. It killed her to have to check the instrument, but there were no other choices. It was times like this she wondered why she didn't play the violin. She could carry that onto the plane.

Relief flooded her as a man brought her the case. She quickly opened it and examined the instrument to assure herself it had arrived in one piece.

Her trip was to last two weeks. She'd wanted to pack only one bag, but against her better judgment, she'd packed two. When the two suitcases dropped to the carousel, she pulled them off and stacked them. One hung from the other, and she slung her carry-on over her shoulder. With a grunt, she hoisted her cello to her side. She started toward the curb to collect a cab.

Footsteps clattered on the tile floor behind her.

"Sophia."

She wouldn't let herself turn to see him hurrying to her.

"Let me help you."

"I travel like this all the time. I do not need your assistance." Her voice was cold.

"I wouldn't be a gentleman if I didn't offer to help a lady in need."

"A gentleman?" He'd already taken her suitcases from her and wheeled them out to the sidewalk. "Mr. Kendal, I assure you I do not need you."

"No, you made that perfectly clear when you disappeared and left your engagement ring in the sink." He kept walking, forcing her to follow.

"Where are you going?" She tried to keep up with him, but his long stride kept him a hefty distance ahead of her.

He pointed off into the parking garage. "My car is parked just over here."

"Your car?" She trotted to catch up with him. "I'm taking a cab."

"I don't want you in a cab in the middle of the night," he said, unwavering from his path.

She grunted and quickened her step again.

"I don't care what you think—"

"I know." He darted a stare in her direction.

"You don't even know where I'm going." She finally closed the distance between them and walked side-by-side with the man who had captured her heart for years. She despised him for it.

"Miss Katie's."

He pushed the button on his key and the lights on the Toyota Camry lit up. "Your cello should fit in the backseat," he said as he hoisted her luggage into the trunk with his own.

Sophia shook her head and opened the back door. She gently laid her cello case across the seat. David shut the trunk and slid past her to open her door. Her breath hitched as the air stirred from his presence.

"Thank you." The words left her mouth without the softness the sentiment should have had.

She dropped into the seat. He winked and shut her

door before walking around to the other side of the car.

"Did you know I was going to be on that flight?" She wondered if she was a victim to a vicious plot to make her face him.

"No." The dip in his voice made her understand that he, too, was disappointed in whatever was going on.

"But you've talked to my grandmother enough to know I'd be here?"

"You forget who her roommate is." He smiled as he drove from the parking garage. "Those two women never stop talking."

"So, how is your Aunt Millie?" She adjusted the scarf at her neck as she peered out the window, awaiting his answer.

"She's fine. She's very happy to be with your grandmother again. You'd think by the way those two carry on that they were little girls and not the eighty-four-year-olds that they are."

"Eighty-three. They won't be eighty-four until next week."

"And that's why you're here." He started up the ramp to the highway.

"Of course. She wants a birthday party. I'm going to make sure she has the best one."

He laughed as she leveled her glance at him.

"What's so funny?"

"Those two will never change. You do realize they've been planning this party for a year. It's all planned out, but I think you are *their* guest of honor."

She shook her head. He had no idea what he talking about. She'd settle into her grandmother's house, and in the morning, they'd have a long talk. If having David at the airport was another attempt at their matchmaking,

Sophia wasn't interested.

"So, you still live in Kansas City?" she asked, watching familiar landmarks pass in the darkness.

"This is home." He turned off the highway and headed down the streets toward her grandmother's house. "What about you? Where do you call home now?"

She didn't like his questioning or maybe it was his tone. Then again, maybe it was because she didn't have an answer for him.

"My apartment is in Seattle."

It wasn't until they headed down the very street where her grandmother lived that Sophia asked, "How is your daughter?"

The words themselves hurt.

"She's wonderful, thank you. She just turned seventeen."

"I'm sure your hands are full with her now." The comment sounded snide, though she hadn't meant it to be.

"She's a good kid. She gets straight A's, she's employee of the month, and a volunteer at the nursing home. She was just elected to the student council, too."

"She makes you very proud." There was a stabbing in her chest and a quiver in her lip. Jealousy was ugly when it reared its head, and she hadn't known she'd still feel it so strongly. Her eyes misted, but she kept them diverted out the window and batted the tears back.

"I'm very proud of her," he said. "You know that her mother left us…left her with me, that is." He slowed the car in front of her grandmother's home. "That was hard on her."

"I'm sure it was."

"Sophia, you can't blame Carissa for what happened to us, if that indeed is what you've done." He pulled the car into the driveway and put it into park.

"I don't." She finally turned toward him and looked him in the eye. "I blame you. I completely blame you. Thank you for the ride." She put her hand on the door to open it, and he caught her other hand in his.

"Sophia, why did you leave?" By his grip on her hand, she knew he'd waited ten years to hear her explanation.

The emotions of the day she'd left flooded back at her, slapping her in the face and squeezing her heart. She hadn't expected to see him today. She hadn't had time to think things out.

She extracted her hand from his and opened the door. She pulled the cello from the backseat as he lifted her suitcases from the trunk and then guided her toward the back porch.

"Why are you going this way?" she whispered, knowing the occupants of the house were asleep.

"Miss Katie doesn't like us to use the front door at night." He took his keys from his pocket and unlocked the door.

"Why do you have a key?" Her voice rose in volume and pitch.

He didn't answer, but pushed open the door and flipped on the light for the enclosed back porch.

David walked in further, turning on the light in the kitchen just through the next door.

It smelled like home. Sophia closed her eyes and soaked it in.

The house had been a boarding house when her grandmother had lived there as a small girl. It had remained one until Sophia was thirteen and her grandfather had died. It was then her grandmother had decided it was no longer safe to live under the same roof with strangers when there was no man to protect them. The decision hadn't disappointed Sophia in the least, though she'd met many wonderful people over the years including a cellist who'd inspired her life's work.

"Are you coming in?" David propped himself against the doorjamb as he watched her.

His lean frame, which stood just shy of six feet, hadn't changed from her memory of him. The face she had known so well had a few lines in places that made her think he'd gotten them from worry. Had he worried about her? No, she decided. He was a father. Fathers, as far as she could remember, had those kinds of lines. The kind of lines that said to the world that they loved someone so much they worried often.

He removed his tie and loosened the buttons on his uniform shirt. Again with a wink, he walked back into the kitchen as she followed with her cello still clutched in her hand.

"You should go now. I'll be just fine. Thank you again for the ride." She laid the instrument across the kitchen table and steadied her eyes on him.

"You always said you'd be fine." He reached into the cupboard for a glass and filled it with water at the sink.

"What does that mean?" Her hands rested on the back of a chair to steady them as she watched his casual actions in her grandmother's kitchen.

"When I asked you to marry me, you said you were fine with the way things were. I bought that. You said you were *fine* not being first seat." He kept his back to her, and she could read tension in the set of his shoulders. "You were *fine* being part of the Kansas City Symphony, and you didn't need to travel or tour with those who asked for you."

"I'm not who I was ten years ago." She crossed her

arms over her chest and let her fingers fidget with the edge of her scarf.

"You sure as hell aren't." He put the glass in the sink and turned to face her.

Their eyes met. He took a step toward her. She could smell him again. His breath caressed her forehead.

He reached a hand to her cheek and brushed it with his thumb. Her breath hitched, and her heart rate quickened. He took another step closer to her until there was no space between them.

Suddenly, she didn't have it in her to fight him.

Gently, ever so gently, he laid a kiss on her lips. Her body swayed toward him. He kept the kiss soft.

A violent storm pulsed through her. He deepened the kiss as he wrapped his arms around her waist and pulled her to him. She still fit. His body was warm against hers, and just like the way she'd felt at home the moment she walked through the back door, she felt at home in his arms.

He rested his forehead against hers. "I've missed you, Sophia Burkhalter."

Then he withdrew his arms from her, and taking a step back, he shoved his hands into his pockets.

"Miss Katie says she'll be making blueberry pancakes in the morning. She usually has breakfast on the table by seven-thirty. I wouldn't be late. I'm sure you know the special pancake breakfast is for you." He walked into the darkened living room.

"Where are you going?" Her heart still pounded in her chest, and her body swayed from his kiss.

David stepped back into the light. A sly smile raised a corner of his mouth, and one of his dark eyebrows arched. She could feel the color rise in her cheeks.

"Oh, that's right. You don't know, do you?" He tapped

his hand on the jamb of the door. "I live here, too. I know you can find your room. It's also where you left it. Good night, Sophia. Sweet dreams."

It was already eight o'clock when the smell of pancakes stirred Sophia awake. She opened her eyes and saw the room of her childhood in the daylight. Warmth filled her, and a smile crossed her lips. She was home.

It had been so long since she'd called anywhere home. She'd known only three in her lifetime. The one she shared for such a short time with her parents. The one she shared with her grandparents after her parents died. She sighed. Then there was the home she'd shared with David.

The thought had tears stinging her eyes and a lump forming in her throat that she forced down. With a deep breath, she cleared her conscience. She'd left. It had been her decision to leave and start a life away from them all. It would be that same life she would return to in fourteen days.

She dug through her suitcase and found her warm, pink robe. She slipped it over her gray pajama bottoms and white tank top. Giving herself a glance in the mirror, she dragged her fingers through her hair and decided there wasn't much she could do with it.

She stood in front of the mirror a moment longer and studied the scar on her neck that had plagued her since childhood. She ran her fingers over it. The hideous mark was there as a reminder of what it had taken to save her life.

Her lips pursed and tears still stung her eyes when she thought about the accident that had put her in the path of death and had taken her parents from her. With one more glance at herself, she tightened up the robe, pulling the lapels together until her throat was covered. Then she headed downstairs.

Chatter came from the kitchen, and Sophia stood on the bottom step and listened. She closed her eyes when she heard her grandmother's voice. Her heart beat faster with the anticipation of her grandmother's arms embracing her. Too many years had passed since she'd seen Katie. Sure, they spoke on the phone every week, but Sophia had been so angry with David and had left in such a storm of emotions that she'd never been back to Kansas City, even to see her grandmother. Guilt that she'd abandoned her to escape humiliation ripped at her. She promised herself to make their time together memorable.

Sophia took a deep breath and walked toward the back of the house to the kitchen. She stopped at the door and watched as her grandmother fussed over pancakes, and Millie stirred together more batter from her seat at the table. David was already up and seated with his aunt. A cup of coffee rested between the palms of his hands. He was dressed in a University of Missouri T-shirt, jeans, and tennis shoes. Obviously, the comfortable attire meant he didn't have to work. The thought had Sophia's heart racing again. He'd be nearby all day.

"Well, well, well. Look who the cat dragged in." Millie noticed Sophia in the doorway and smiled.

"Good morning, Ms. Millie." She walked to the table and kissed her on the cheek. Then she turned to her grandmother, who waited for her with damp eyes. "Good morning, Grandma." She wrapped her arms around the woman who had meant so much in her life. They clung to each other for a long time.

Katie Burkhalter held her granddaughter at arm's length and took in the sight of her. "Oh, my little Sophie, look at you. You're more beautiful than I remember." She smiled and pulled her close again. "I've missed you," she whispered.

"I've missed you ,too." Her voice wobbled. David crossed the room to the coffeepot, and she hoped he was too busy to notice her emotional greeting with her grandmother.

"You look like you could use this." He was standing behind her. She turned, and he held out a cup of coffee to her.

"Thank you." She took the cup without looking up at him.

Millie smiled from beyond her bowl of blueberries and batter. Her soft, blue eyes shimmered with mischief.

"What a coincidence that you were both on the same plane."

"Who said we were?" David raised his eyebrows at his aunt as she exchanged a glance with Katie.

They were at it again. Sophia shook her head, and Katie looked too innocent.

"Oh, hush." Katie pushed Sophia toward the table and laid a plate of pancakes in front of her. "Eat, you're too skinny."

"Oh, Grandma, you're the only one who would think so." Sophia laughed as David slid into the seat next to her and looked her over.

"I think she's right." He watched her from over the top of his coffee mug. "I don't remember you looking so frail."

"Frail?" Her mouth was full of pancake, but her heart was full of fury. She washed down the bite with her coffee and took a breath to give David a piece of her mind. At the last second, she bit it back, not wanting to upset her grandmother or Millie.

"So, did you two have time to talk last night? Did you

make up? Everything back to the way it was?" Millie asked with as much enthusiasm as she possessed in her tiny body.

"Aunt Millie, things between me and Sophie have been over for a very long time," David replied.

A surge of two very different emotions went through her. First, the fact that he'd admitted things were over between them, which they were, infuriated her. That should have been what she'd gotten to say to drive home the point even harder after they'd somehow managed to get them on the same flight.

Then a gentle calm took over when she realized he'd called her Sophie. She lifted her mug to her lips to hide the smile she had surfaced when he'd called her that. It was the name those who loved her called her. The memory of him calling her Sophie had spiked a jolt of happiness through her she didn't know still existed.

The fluttering of happiness lasted only a moment and faded quickly when Sophia watched the figure of a young woman walk into the kitchen. Her long, straight, dark hair hung past her shoulders and over her face. Her shoulders hunched as she shuffled her bunny-clad feet across the kitchen floor. She had on nothing more than her tank top and a pair of cut-off sweatpants.

Black fingernail polish, half chipped off, coated her nails, and at least twelve black rubber bracelets adorned her.

The girl shuffled to the coffeepot, poured herself a cup of coffee, and then shuffled back out and up the stairs without one word muttered to anyone in the room.

David raised his mug as if to salute his daughter with it. "And now you've met Carissa."

All the joy in Sophia's body drained. Resentment for the man whose face had haunted her since she'd walked out on him overtook her. She turned back to her coffee. It had gone cold.

She'd met Carissa before. Perhaps he'd forgotten. It had been mere days before she'd decided to walk out of his life.

In fact, Sophia had been the one who opened the door that day.

Standing before her was a little girl with matted braids and dirty clothes. Sophia was sure she was there to sell them something, but the child looked up at her and said, "I'm looking for David Kendal. I'm his daughter."

Tears stung Sophia's eyes when she thought of it. David had dropped to his knees in front of little girl when he'd seen her. She'd whispered in his ear, and he'd embraced her. Moments later, they were running out the door without Sophia to help the little girl's mother. There had been the one phone call from David asking her to come to the hospital, saying he couldn't leave. She'd gone, just as he'd asked her to do, even though her heart had been broken. She'd stood just beyond the room looking in. A woman lay in the bed, a doctor attended to her, and David sat with Carissa on his lap, her head on his shoulder. She'd taken one step toward the room when a nurse had stopped her and told her that no one could go in except the *husband* and the daughter. Sophia left two days later. She couldn't stand the deception.

The man she loved was a father and obviously, according to the nurse, someone else's husband. She'd decided at that moment she didn't need anyone like that in her life. She'd be *fine*. Just as David had said she was.

Meet the Author

Damon Kappel ©2009

Bestselling Author Bernadette Marie is known for building families readers want to be part of. Her series *The Keller Family* has graced bestseller charts since its release in 2011, along with her other series and single title books. The married mother of five sons promises *Happily Ever After always*...and says she can write it, because she lives it.

When not writing, Bernadette Marie is shuffling her sons to their many events—mostly hockey—and enjoying the beautiful views of the Colorado Rocky Mountains from her front step. She is also an accomplished martial artist with a second degree black belt in Tang Soo Do.

A chronic entrepreneur, Bernadette Marie opened her own publishing house in 2011, *5 Prince Publishing,* so that she could publish the books she liked to write and help make the dreams of other aspiring authors come true too.

CPSIA information can be obtained at www.ICGtesting.com
Printed in the USA
LVOW07s2145181114

414431LV00001B/47/P

9 781631 120435